ALFONSO

Also by Felix Calvino

A Hatful of Cherries

ALFONSO

Félix Calvino

ARCADIA

The Press On series of novels was founded by Michael Wilding and Phillip Edmonds. Edmonds was the managing director of *Wet Ink*, the magazine of new writing, and Wilding is Press On's commissioning editor.

Press On – 20

First published 2013 by Arcadia
the general books' imprint of
Australian Scholarly Publishing Pty Ltd
7 Little Lothian Street Nth, North Melbourne Vic. 3051
TEL: 03 9329 6963 FAX: 03 9329 5452
EMAIL: aspic@ozemail.com.au WEB: scholarly.info

ISBN: 978-1-925003-20-8

A Catloguing-in-Publication entry is available
from the National Library of Australia.

Cover design Sarah Anderson
Design and typesetting Art Rowlands
Printing and binding Tenderprint Pty Ltd

Set in Fairfield LH 45 Light 11.7pt

For my grandchildren
Isabella, Sebastián, Julia, Román, and Lucía

Part One

Chapter 1

It was mid October but the jacarandas were not yet in bloom due to a lingering winter. Alfonso was walking home from his job at a construction site and wishing he had a girlfriend when he saw her at the bus stop outside the Water Board head office. A second look at her long, straight black hair, pale face, and wide mouth left him with no doubt that she was the perfect double of a girl he had once admired very much in his village in Galicia. Alfonso was twenty-three and had been in Sydney for almost a year.

Excitement and confusion remained with him throughout the afternoon. He thought back to the village girl all evening, the next day, and the day after that. Mostly, his mind returned to one of the rare occasions he had talked to her. It took place immediately after their First Communion, when they were both ten or eleven years old and all the communing children had been invited to the priest's residence beside the church. There they received small bags of sweets and an image of the Virgin Mary and baby Jesus. The village girl, dressed in white and looking more angel than girl, had walked with him, remaining beside him during the gathering. He could not recall what they said to each other, but he remembered feeling nervous while chewing his sweets quickly and noisily. Just as they were leaving the priest's courtyard to join their parents, she had given him some of hers.

In his memory, he returned to that church square. His mother, two aunties, and a cousin were embracing him. His brother stood a little apart, eying a group of girls nearby. It was the feast of St Maria, the village's patron saint, so the square was crowded with children, parents, neighbours and relatives, all dressed in their best. The village band was playing traditional tunes, favourites of the not-so-young. Afterwards, they would play some dance music for those who could not wait for the evening section to show off their dancing skills. The annual fiesta was always a good day, but this year was special, he thought, as his hand caressed the three wrapped sweets melting in his pocket.

He recalled the years at their village school, and his dreaming of her across a space guarded by her parents' eighteen cows and one horse, and her two older brothers. She went to college in the city, returning each summer and Christmas, more a woman, and further out of reach. These were days of turmoil, of mortifying memories of poverty, of insecurity, of having to accept that she would never be his. Now the old, long-suppressed fantasies began to revive and interact with the new.

Within two days he had devised a plan to meet with the replica girl. On Saturday, thinking that she might also have been on her way home from work, he hurried to the same bus stop, sat at one end of the bench, and unfolded a newspaper. She arrived five minutes later and joined two women who were already there. They spoke about one thing and another. The older of the two women pulled out a Beatles record she had just bought. It started to rain, so the three friends moved under the bus shelter. She was so close he could touch her. She wore a black miniskirt and a white blouse with a logo from the local Walton's store on the breast pocket.

The bus arrived, and she and her friends climbed aboard. The bus pulled away, and he sat there for a while, rejoicing in his good fortune.

The next Saturday, Alfonso requested permission from his supervisor to leave half an hour early. There was not a cloud in the sky, and the breeze was cool and fresh. A good omen, he thought as he walked down Clarence Street to the Town Hall. He sat on the marble steps in front of the building and looked around. It was a popular meeting place. A smartly dressed middle-aged man on his right constantly checked his watch and combed his hair. A couple of steps below, two pretty women cocked their heads right and left, like sparrows between drinks.

Time passed slowly for Alfonso, his eyes fixed on the main entrance to Walton's department store. When the Town Hall clock struck twelve, he knew that the moment he longed for was approaching. He would invite her to the cinema. There would be no mocking boys or tittering girls around her, as there had been with the girl in the village. Still, he was perspiring a little.

She emerged at twenty past the hour. He rose to his feet, waited for a break in the traffic, and hurried across George Street. He caught up with her at the red light on the corner of Bathurst and Pitt.

'Pardon, Miss…'

She turned her head. 'What do you want?'

'I'd like you to come with me to …'

'And I'd like you to get lost,' she hissed.

The traffic signal changed to green.

Alfonso remained motionless for a minute or two and then walked slowly towards Paddy's Market. His legs felt weak, as if he had just emerged from a long illness. His hands were moist and his face and ears were cold. He had no name for his other sensations. He bought cheese, salami, sardines, chicken legs, and pork chops. Today he did not care to compare prices or search for specials. The commotion of the markets overwhelmed him, but on the way out, the promotional shouting of a greengrocer attracted his attention and he ended up with a twenty-kilo bag of potatoes at a heavily discounted price.

Outside, the sun was high and unusually hot. He trudged up Commonwealth Street to Palmer, staring at the ground ahead of him. He was vaguely aware that the traffic, both cars and pedestrians, was already slowing down for the weekend. He stopped often to move the bag of potatoes from one shoulder to the other.

At home, he organised the meat into daily portions for the freezer and put the other goods away. He lay on the couch for his usual Saturday afternoon rest, and the corresponding feeling of relaxation that came with the beginning of the weekend, but he couldn't doze off, not even with a pillow over his face. He got up and took the laundry bag to the laundromat adjacent to ABC House on William Street. While the machine moaned and spun through its cycles, he leafed through the pages of the *Daily Telegraph*, hardly reading the words. When a young couple asked him for the cinema section, he gave them the entire paper and gazed at the colours tumbling in the tall dryers.

Back home, after he folded and put away the washing, he kept busy sweeping and mopping the linoleum floor and cleaning the small kitchen and the bathroom. Despite all this activity, he could not forget the girl's words at the traffic lights, or erase the image of her eyes, cold and unblinking, staring at him.

In bed that night, completely awake, he reasoned that his imperfect English had turned her away.

In the morning he pretended that the incident never happened. But during his lunch break on Monday, he asked his fellow carpenters—migrants mostly—if anyone knew of a place where he could learn to speak English properly. Richard stared at him as he slowly chewed his egg sandwich. Domenico suggested that a woman giving lessons in bed was the best.

The local English classes for migrants were held at Rushcutters Bay Public School on Monday evenings. Besides Alfonso, thirteen others attended—seven men and six women. At twenty-three, Alfonso was the youngest man there. He was also in trouble, as he hardly knew what nouns, verbs, and adjectives were. Doña Concepción, his village schoolteacher, had taught him to read and write and to do some arithmetic. There had been no room for anything else.

But he had a good memory and he could reproduce the sounds that he heard, a skill he had perfected as a child, imitating birdcalls while grazing their two cows. Now, in Sydney, this old pastime allowed him to reproduce the tone and nuance of English words just as they came from the teacher's mouth, bringing instant laughter to the class and a puzzled look to her face.

He discovered that he liked to read, a practice that in time became habitual. On the advice of the teacher, Anne, he bought his first dictionary and took out a year's subscription to *Reader's Digest*. The dictionary and the magazines became his prized possessions. One taught him the meaning of words, the other the purpose of things. He had been most impressed with pictures of the human brain nesting within the skull, and articles about the mechanical functions of the heart and the bellows inside the lungs, all clothed in skin for protection and privacy. He thought of the ears and the nose, and how little he really knew of anything.

He also began to realise the importance of having a command of language. He wanted more than the mutilated English that met the needs of the workplace and brought him some success with Australian girls. Language, he reasoned, was both an entry and a barrier to the Australian universe located outside his circle of workmates and Spanish-speaking friends.

But learning it proved difficult. His memory, amenable to the retention of sound, resented having to carry a second label for meaning and a third for the spelling of every new word. He had to rely on brute repetition. The only thing that kept him going was the thought of Carla, a girl who also attended the evening classes. Tall and slim, with the gentlest face he had ever known, she had brown eyes and hay-coloured hair hanging loose over her shoulders, or in two braids draped over her small breasts. She was twenty-two years old.

At first, they exchanged furtive glances across the classroom. Then they sat together at a desk carved with names, arrowed hearts, and forgotten dates, and together watched the teacher roll her tongue to illustrate the birth of English sound. After class, he accompanied her to the bus, which, to his dismay, was always on time.

In the last class before Christmas, the teacher emphasised in her calm voice the importance of reading, writing down new words, and repeating them until they were embedded in the memory. The class presented her with a box of chocolates and a big card, and someone proposed that they all go for a drink at a nearby hotel.

As they were leaving the classroom, Carla whispered to Alfonso that she was expected home. In front of the school, the class departed in one direction, Alfonso and Carla in the other. They walked slowly, almost touching. The night was warm and humid. Irregular sounds of a school band practice reached them. Alfonso wanted to ask her for a date, but the recent incident crossed his mind and he held his tongue. He pointed instead to the fruit bats flying high in the early evening sky and told her how in his village, he and his school friends would smoke bats out of their caves. She wanted to know why they had done that. He was not sure. Carla's bus appeared around the corner, they ran for it, and she got in. Through the open window, they looked into each other's eyes until the bus pulled away. Within minutes he was cursing himself for words left unsaid, and he felt hopeless for many days.

Carla did not return to classes the following year. Alfonso's request for her phone number was brusquely rejected by the school's enrolment office.

A week or so into the new year, Alfonso remembered the teacher's advice and decided to join the public library. A couple of weeks later, just before the midday break, a scaffold worker was badly hurt and work was suspended for the day. On his way home, Alfonso stopped at the Pitt Street branch of the library, found a copy of the *Telegraph* and a Spanish-English dictionary, and went in search of a table. He avoided the big reading tables, with people flicking through pages and irritating him, and chose a small one by the window. It offered a view of people waiting at the traffic lights or jostling one another, a way for him to escape when weariness set in from looking up new words.

He sat down. As he bent to search his bag for word cards and a pencil, he saw a large book leaning against the wall. He picked it up and opened it.

Within an hour, he had seen all the oceans and continents of the world through the pages of a *Times Atlas*. Previously, New Zealand, Montevideo, Nova Scotia, as well as the biblical places Father Manuel repeated every Sunday, had been just names to Alfonso, cities or countries scattered at random on the surface of a globe he could not envision. And in the map of the universe, he saw that the earth was round and floated miraculously in space, a concept that until then he only vaguely understood.

Walking home from the library that afternoon, Alfonso reflected on his newly discovered overview of the Earth and its near and distant neighbours. Although he did not understand the mechanics of what kept the planets turning in such splendid harmony, he thought it was all quite marvellous. But later the same day, realising how far away he was from the village, once the centre of his world, it disturbed and saddened him. Later still, he thought of the names and places along the route of that month-long journey from his village to Australia and wanted to know their geographical position on the big world map. So a week later he returned to the library, sat down in front of the atlas, and with one finger on the page and an eye on his memory, he began to recreate his journey to Australia two years earlier.

It was a Saturday afternoon in early February of 1962, when he arrived in the northwest Galician city of Ourense, the first city he had ever seen. At the railway station, he was informed he had four hours to wait for his train. He'd thought that four hours was forever and wandered outside, but he did not go far. Wind and low clouds threatened late winter rain. The streets were crowded, and the buildings, taller than the village church bell tower, made him feel small. Besides, he was tired from carrying his suitcase five kilometres from the village to the bus stop on the main road.

Back at the station's waiting area, he made the acquaintance of a sparrow and an elderly pigeon. He crumbed some cheese and bread for them, and they ate dinner together. It grew dark outside and his new friends departed. He kept an eye on the slow-turning hands of the station clock and let his thoughts return to the village and the silent sadness of his mother and his brother eating soup and bread at the kneading trough that served as a dining table. In the wood basket, Angelina and her two kittens would be sleeping. On the ceiling, the flies would have settled in for the night.

He already missed his mother. He missed his brother, too. He remembered, with grief, his brother labouring like a man when he was still a boy, struggling to supplement their living from several small plots of land, two cows, three beehives, one pig, and half a dozen hens. He had delighted in showing Alfonso how to trap foxes and rabbits, and to fish for trout. Mother would sell their catch to buy oil, sugar, and things for the house. When he was eight or nine, Alfonso discovered the secret universe of dreams and the soothing effect of prayer. He called on both for help in catching trout and fat hares, and for his brother to have plenty of labouring jobs. It did not happen, but they managed not to go cold or hungry, their clothes were always clean and carefully mended, and they were comfortable in being themselves.

His finger moved across the atlas's pages towards León. It had been slow going for the train, crawling through tunnels in the mountains and stopping at every station. Then came Irún at the French border. Alfonso was impressed with the ease with which he had navigated the entire length of Spain. But achievement came at a price, and his heart ached again, just as it did when he embraced his mother and brother before leaving the house.

Irún to Paris was a fast journey. When the train stopped at Bordeaux, he looked out the window and saw a married couple walking on the platform with their two young daughters. Shortly after, they entered his compartment and checked their tickets against the numbered seats. The mother sat by the window opposite him, with the lovely girls beside her. The husband said something to Alfonso and he replied, 'No comprendo'. The women smiled and their kind expressions and scents caressed his senses. One by one, the women switched off their reading lights. The husband folded his newspaper and went out. Alfonso woke from a deep sleep to a silvery light coming through the train window. He didn't know where he was and closed his eyes again. Just then the husband reappeared, drunk, and it would be daylight before peace was restored to the compartment.

At Calais, he saw the sea and black people for the first time. Wind and rain pelted the ferry's windows during the crossing of the English Channel, and he felt sick to his stomach.

In Victoria Station, Alfonso stood on the concourse, his suitcase beside him. People milled around and strode past him, speaking languages he did not understand. He felt overwhelmed. Then two men stopped nearby, close enough for him to hear what they were saying.

'*Envíame una postal,*' said one. 'Send me a postcard.'

'*Y tú cuídame los peces,*' answered the other. 'And you take care of my fish.'

They embraced warmly. Alfonso waited for one man to go through the departure gate before approaching the other.

This fellow Spaniard, whose name was Ovidio, not only showed Alfonso where to catch the train to Southampton, but also paid for several cups of coffee and a large plate of fish and chips—a most welcome change after two days of bread, cheese, and salted pork from his knapsack. A kind man, Alfonso thought, not knowing yet that in foreign lands the bond of common language made instant friends out of strangers.

Ovidio had lived in France for eleven years, and in England for nineteen. He envied Alfonso for his trip to Australia, and José, the friend he had just driven to the station, for his holiday in Spain.

'Now I am stuck here, finished,' he said.

Ovidio had seemed relaxed but now he looked gloomy.

'Why?' Alfonso asked, immediately regretting it as an improper question.

Ovidio remained silent for a while, his hands half-covering his face. Then he lit a cigarette and went on. 'It was the third of April, 1939. The Civil War had ended two days earlier and I was on my way back to my family, still dressed in the uniform of the losing side since I couldn't afford to buy other clothes. I came in sight of a large town and decided to bypass it. I took a path that followed the river and that's where I stumbled on the still-warm bodies of two men, both of them civilians.

'How a photographer was there to record me removing the shoes of one corpse and the trousers of another I will never know. Many years passed before I was cleared of murder and by then I had sworn not to return to Spain while Franco lived.'

Alfonso did not tell Ovidio that his father had been killed, murdered according to some, in the same war.

The train from London arrived at Southampton at noon. At three in the afternoon, Alfonso boarded the ocean liner *Fairstar*, located his cabin, put his suitcase under his bunk, and returned to the deck. By now, passengers were tied to families and friends on the dock with coloured streamers. A whistle sounded. The ship began to move. As the streamers became taut, a collective sadness spread through the people. Alfonso also waved, and his eyes filled with tears for those whose faces were not in the crowd.

Rain and rough seas for the first two days had produced much vomiting among the passengers, until calm returned. Now, on the map before him he saw the Portuguese coast, the eastward turn into the Mediterranean, Port Said, where they had stopped for a day, the slender Suez Canal, with just sand on both sides, the Red Sea, another stop at Aden on the Arabian Peninsula, and after that, the long Indian Ocean stretch to the city of Fremantle, in Western Australia.

He clearly recalled the screeching seagulls above his head, the unsteady feeling in his legs, and the mixed excitement and hesitation in his mind as he stood on solid ground again.

'The library will close in ten minutes. Thank you,' a soft female voice said from a speaker in the ceiling. He returned his notebook and pencil to his bag, the atlas to the bookshelf, and went out. He thought back to the voyage's early days, which began with a breakfast feast of eggs, bacon, cereals, toast, and fruit. The lunch buffet stretched the length of the room, containing more varieties of meats, salads, and cheeses than he had seen in his entire life. And after these feasts, dinner was still to come.

The simple happiness from a full stomach and a rested body had started to ebb by the end of the first week. On the decks, in the dining room, at the cinema, everywhere he went, there were unfamiliar people who spoke only English. In his cabin, the ship's engines growled and shuddered beneath his bunk. His two companions, both New Zealanders, often argued late into the night. Halfway through the journey, they settled their argument, whatever it was, but it seemed to Alfonso that their snoring was even louder. And he was tormented by his own dumb silence and wondered who he was and what he would become, torn from all that what was known to him.

That anxiety lifted after the half-day stopover at Fremantle but returned a few days later as they approached Sydney. The last night on board, he awoke at two in the morning. The feeling of apprehension, maybe fear, was too strong for him to go back to sleep.

After a while he got up. Taking care not to wake his companions, he dressed, and went to the top deck. There stars were bright and the sea calm. Unable to keep still, he paced the deck backwards and forwards. He recalled in the village that time when he got a lift to town with the local veterinarian. They spoke about the lack of work locally, and how young men were making their way to other countries. Alfonso mentioned that he was considering doing the same. The vet said the enforced exile of so many young men and women was a shame. He advised Alfonso not to go to France or Germany or any other European country, because they offered only temporary residential permits and had a poor opinion of guest workers. He said he should stay clear of the old stamping grounds of Argentina, Panama, and Venezuela, with their routine revolutions, and the continual readjustment from having enough to get by one day, to being penniless the next. Canada and Australia, he said, were the only decent places left. But the one was always cold and the other was very far away.

It was noon when Alfonso disembarked at Circular Quay. His sponsor, Raul, waited for him by the public telephones. About forty-five, sad-eyed, and sporting a small moustache, Raul wore a Basque beret and carried a folded newspaper under his arm. Alfonso approached him. They shook hands.

'How was the trip?' Raul asked as they walked to his car.

'Good, but interminably long,' replied Alfonso, glad to hear and to speak his own language.

'Yes, it's a long trip. But you are here now.'

'Thank you for sending me the papers.'

'That is what family is for, Alfonso.'

'Do you like it here?

'There is plenty of work. And it is possible to save money. But the language is a big problem for us. We are planning to go home in three or four years' time.'

Raul was silent for the rest of the fifteen-minute drive to his house in Paddington. Alfonso thought about what Raul had said, and looked out the window at the different cars on the road. Perhaps one day he would have a car of his own.

Raul's wife, Remedios, served fish and salad for lunch, roast lamb and vegetables for dinner. She asked Alfonso many questions, including the cost of milk and bread back in Spain.

The following morning, Raul showed him the city's best-known sites, including the flying boats at Rose Bay and the Opera House under construction. In the evening, they went to the Spanish Club. After dinner, Raul proposed, and a friend of his seconded, Alfonso's application for membership. The committee man on duty explained that the club's purpose was to provide a home away from home for its members. He mentioned the various social and cultural activities available, including Spanish classes for the children of members.

That night in bed, Alfonso thought that the events of the last two days seemed hazy, like the backdrop of an old photograph. But the kindness of Raul and Remedios was clear. And the Spanish Club, a place to escape from the silence that had troubled him on the ship, was also reassuring.

At six-thirty the following morning, Raul drove him to a near-finished apartment building in Bondi Junction. There they met the builder who had provided the required work guarantee. Two hours later, Alfonso was at work on the site, hanging doors and affixing locks, architraves, and skirting boards. The job was over in a month, but another one was found for him with a construction company where he would remain for many years.

Three months later, feeling he should have his own place, he found a room with a tiny kitchen, shower, and toilet on the first floor of a red brick building between a hardware store and a fenced-off empty lot at the lower end of William Street. Raul provided the references the estate agents required for the landlord. And Remedios, after a brief inspection of the place, presented him with two sets of bed linen, an array of pots and pans, some knives and forks. Her parting gift, the day he left, was a large bowl of potato and beef stew.

Months stretched into a year. The Circular Quay building where he was working was completed and Alfonso moved on to a new site in Macquarie Street. In those days new buildings were going up everywhere. One Friday evening in early December he went to the Spanish Club to renew his membership. Afterwards at the bar, Fidel, a friend of Raul's, invited him to his table to meet his wife Maria, her cousin Eulalia, and another couple. Alfonso sat next to Eulalia. They talked. She was from a village in the mountains in Asturias, had been in Australia for seven months, and worked in the kitchens of Parliament House. She had a pale face, hair tucked behind her ears, and eyes the colour of chestnuts. She smelled of mimosa.

They had another drink before going upstairs to the

dance floor. A popular orchestra was playing and the place was full, but they managed to squeeze around a friend's table. Alfonso and Eulalia danced before the floorshow and again after. She refused to dance with anyone else. Past midnight, Eulalia's cousin complained of a headache; shortly afterwards, they left. Outside the club, Fidel offered Alfonso a lift, but he politely refused. It was a favourite routine for him to walk home from the club on Saturday evenings.

Walking up Liverpool Street, he recalled the faces of the girls he danced with and of those he'd wished to. On Elizabeth Street, he glanced at the tall buildings, their glass facades now grey. Across the road, Hyde Park was speckled by pale circles of light below the lamps.

On Cathedral Street, he admired the imposing stone structure of the Museum of Natural Science. His mind strayed to the big dinosaur on the ground floor, and to the displays on the floors above. All dead things, the secret spaces in their hearts empty, yet free from cold and hunger; they would be more comfortable now than when they were alive, he thought.

At Palmer and Crown, he acknowledged the greetings from the girls with red mouths standing in dimly-lit doorways, offering instant love at giveaway prices. Home was on the other side of William Street, in the suburb named Woolloomooloo, the spelling of which always tested his patience, though he liked the sound.

But tonight he had a companion on his familiar journey. A part of him was still on the dance floor, his hand on Eulalia's long straight spine, the motion of her hips against his, her words and gestures spreading through his brain.

Arriving home, he drank a glass of water, standing at the sink in front of the window and staring into the dark.

Talking and dancing with Eulalia had left him confused and flattered at the same time. Often he gazed at the poster of Raquel Welch or the *Daily Mirror*'s Page 3 girls adorning the walls of the lunchroom at work, and asked himself if it would be possible to live beside so much splendour. Now, though it had the quality of a dream, it could be for real, he thought as he hung his going-out clothes in the cupboard.

In the weeks ahead, he and Eulalia met every Saturday, but always in the company of friends. One Sunday afternoon, three months into their unspoken courtship, they went to the cinema. Afterwards, in the gathering dusk, they strolled through Hyde Park and sat on a park bench. She said she had liked the movie and wished she could understand English. She said she would never be able to learn English because she worked with Italians and lived with Spaniards. He offered to share with her what he knew of the language. It would be good for him also, as he had limited chance to practice. And he would take her to the cinema whenever she wanted. She said she would like that and took his hand.

The light of a waxing moon rising behind St Mary's Cathedral filtered through the leaves and made weird patterns on their faces. They looked at each other and laughed. Their lips met, gently at first. After a while, they sought shelter in the shadows of the Cenotaph and lay on the grass. Both shaking, both unsure how to proceed, he unbuttoned her blouse, felt her breasts, her silvery belly. She fumbled at his belt.

Alfonso believed some things should be forgotten. But that humiliating experience—when it mattered most, nerves took over and he could not deliver—would remain with him for a long time.

Twelve months passed, and another twelve. Alfonso still worked at the Macquarie Street site. The flow of seasons was vague, hard to see where one ended and another one began. Yet even a small difference in temperature was sufficient to start him longing for the old village seasons. He thought of how each season brought change. In Spain, spring painted the world green and filled the air with the smell of freshly ploughed fields. Long summer days of rye harvesting and haymaking were followed by dances in the evening. In autumn there were mists, yellow leaves, ripe corn, and chestnuts. Winter brought short days, cold rain, bitter frost, and deathlike silence to woods weighed down with snow.

The fishing tackle shop next to the Haymarket Library always set into motion the most terrible homesickness, for those hours spent trout fishing in the mountain rivers were marked, in his heart, as the most contented of his life.

These snapshots in Alfonso's memory—pages in a picture book, he called them—represented the remnants of his old world. In the new world, there were pages but no pictures. Memory pictures needed the glue of emotion to stick, and in Australia, he had none. At work he measured, cut, and nailed concrete moulds from plywood from seven until four, Monday to Friday and eight to twelve on Saturdays.

A relentless sameness, momentarily broken by the long weekends of Easter, Christmas, and the Queen's Birthday, left his body rested but his mind agitated. He thought of it as a fever he would have to learn to live with. There was no going back. By an unspoken rule of the village, as old as the village well, it was acceptable to leave and prosper. Return only if you succeed.

No. He could not let his yearnings for the past infect the present. He must always remember the despair of his youth, the prospect of a life trapped in the bleakness of potato and cabbage soup, wooden shoes, and re-mended corduroy trousers.

He was now living in Sydney, a faraway place he had once heard of but never expected to visit. And for the first time in his life he was on his own, independent, a grown-up man. His working conditions and wages were decent. The bed-sitter he rented was on the first floor of a building containing similar dwellings. It had a couch that became a bed, a clothes cupboard, two chairs and a table, a fridge, gas stove, a shower, and a toilet. There was a partial view of Woolloomooloo Bay from the small window above the sink. The sun flooded the room on its way up, the moon at night. It was clear to him that the pain of nostalgia paralysed him, and if left unguarded, might ruin this new life of his that provided all he needed and more than he had ever expected. And he could draw on the future. Sometimes, at the edge of sleep, he had sensed the beginning of joy taking form in the shape of a house and a woman.

Meanwhile, he carried out the demands of his job meticulously, embraced overtime, and saved, without being overly thrifty. In the evenings, he cooked dinner and watched the six o'clock news, switching off the pictures of the Vietnam War, as they reminded him of another war, from which his father had never returned. He read and wrote new words on white cards and said them out loud when he was on his own.

On Saturdays, he finished work at twelve and did the weekly shopping on the way back. In the afternoon, after a siesta on the couch, he tidied the place a little, polished his shoes, and ironed a shirt and trousers. Near evening, he went to the Spanish Club.

At the restaurant, he would meet with Eladio, the tailor with the shy smile who thought coming to Australia was the biggest mistake of his life.

'Can you imagine travelling so far for so little?' he said to Alfonso late one night at a café in Kings Cross. 'In Toledo, I had a girlfriend whose feelings and language I understood. I was a junior partner in a good business. My clients made themselves available for one measuring and two fittings. Here they call me 'the cutter.' I cut for large, medium, and small ghosts. In the floor below, an army of women stitch the pieces together. Mr Silverman visits in the morning and the afternoon to remind everybody that "time is money."'

They would be joined by Julián and the brothers Ramirez, the handsome twins with black, hypnotic eyes, who thought of the weekend as the season of love. After a drink or two, they would take a taxi to the Concordia or the Apia Club, or a place their scouts had recommended. Alfonso had misgivings about these excursions, but the Spanish Club dance floor, with Eulalia and her friends sitting among the crowd, was not an attractive option.

Usually Alfonso's friends paired up and he hailed a taxi home alone. On the occasions when he felt jealous or frustrated, he reassured himself that, by the law of averages, his turn was bound to come someday.

On Sundays, when he was not doing small jobs for a builder friend or his plumber friend, he changed the bed linen, hung out the laundry, and cleaned his room.

Once in a while he visited a small stone church near Central Station that had heavy, oak doors and smelled of candle wax. He had been quite religious as a boy. Not now. But he saw no harm in going. The Mass was in Spanish, and Father José preached short sermons about gentle Jesus and mercy for those who had lost their way. This was a welcome change from the lurid details of hell and purgatory awaiting the sinners in the afterlife, which had been the predominant theme of Don Manuel, the old village priest. The church building had beautifully assembled redwood ceilings, and by sitting in one of the pews at the back, Alfonso had a good view of the saints and angels in the seven stained-glass windows. It was different than his old village church, which was built entirely of stone and was always cold, even in summer.

Then his thoughts would turn to the time, still firmly affixed in his memory, when his devotion began to sink. Amador, his school and fishing companion since childhood, fell in love with a local girl. After her parents had failed to convince her that she deserved a better man, they sought the priest's assistance, and Amador was required to memorise the Our Father, The Creed, and Holy Mary. He failed twice, but succeeded the third time. The priest then added the Seven Deadly Sins and the Ten Commandments. The learning and relearning went on for a year-and-a-half. It finished on St Peter's Day, when during the fireworks the couple sneaked away, walked three kilometres to the Roman bridge, and jumped to the dark waters below.

Alfonso remembered another woman from those early Sydney days. One evening, returning from buying the weekly Spanish paper on Darlinghurst Road, he felt thirsty and went into the Orange Spot. He was at the counter, waiting for his pineapple juice. She asked him for a lighter, and he borrowed one from the man behind the juice machine. Afterwards they sat on stools and talked at a little counter that ran along one of the walls.

Her English was difficult, her accent pleasing. She was

from Noumea, New Caledonia; tall, serene, and dressed in white linen. She had short black hair, a lovely mouth, white teeth, and smooth skin almost as brown as her chocolate eyes. When she finished her cigarette, Alfonso suggested they go to his place, a short distance away, for a wine or coffee. Yes, she would like a wine. Could they buy matches and cigarettes on the way? A beautiful woman, he thought, as they walked down William Street.

At his place, in the faint light from the cream-colored lamp on top of the fridge, he put together a snack of bread and cheese, salami, olives, and wine. She ate and drank a little, smoked constantly. Classic dance music was playing on the radio, and, at her request, they got up from the table and danced. They kissed.

Then she was silent, her smile vanished, and her eyes appeared to be looking at something not in the room. He tried to comfort her with wine and black coffee. Neither helped. Shortly after, she said she was in Australia to have an abortion.

'You, by yourself?'

'Yes.'

'Could he not …'

'He is a fake.'

'Your family?'

'They would kill me.'

She started to cry, and he pulled out the sofa bed. She buried her face in the pillow. Sobs shook her body. He sat on the edge of the bed and gently patted her back as he had seen mothers do to lull their babies to sleep.

Then she was calm.

Alfonso covered her with a blanket, turned the radio down, and poured himself a glass of wine.

Half an hour or so later, she got up.

'May I use your bathroom?' she asked, her voice a little husky.

'Of course,' Alfonso replied and pointed to the only other door in the room. While she was gone, he cleared the table and lit the Kookaburra burner to boil water for coffee.

'Can I get you something to drink?' he asked when she came out.

'Just a glass of water, thank you,' she said and tried to smile.

She sat at the table, took a sip, and lit a cigarette. She looked at her wristwatch and then at him.

They left soon after. On William Street, he hailed a taxi. They both sat in the back in silence during the short drive to her hotel on Macleay Street. The briefest of kisses sealed their encounter.

On his return, Alfonso was greeted by a trace of her perfume still in the room, and he liked it very much. Soon it would be more than five years since he had arrived in Australia to escape poverty. He had friends, a good job, and substantial savings in the bank. He had conquered the language barrier and the pangs of longing for his village. But his good fortune did not extend to women.

He brushed his teeth and undressed for bed. Her scent on the pillow was especially strong. It was here that her tears and memories had mingled. He wished this lovely but troubled woman who had come and gone and whose name he did not know all the luck in the word. And he wished for a little love for himself.

Part Two

Chapter 1

'A deceased estate … enormous potential for improvements … a typical worker's terrace cottage built in the 1880s' were some of the phrases the real estate agent from L. J. Hooker had repeated many times at the supervisor's barbecue. The man had annoyed Alfonso for two hours. Alfonso distrusted people who talked too much. They reminded him of gypsies selling horses.

Yet he did not dismiss the agent's words. Owning a home had been a recurring dream, and so he attended the 'open for inspection' of 10 Charles Street, Surry Hills, the following Saturday.

It was a narrow house on a narrow street of five identical houses, joined by common walls. A spiked wrought-iron fence and a tiny patio separated it from the sidewalk. Two concrete steps led to the front door. Inside, there were two rooms to the left of the hallway, and the kitchen was at the back. Beyond the kitchen were the bathroom, laundry, and a small backyard. Steep, narrow stairs led to three bedrooms. In the larger front room, French doors opened to a verandah overlooking the street.

It needs much work, he reasoned on the way back to the bed-sitter. But that was alright. Then, late in the afternoon, a sense of hesitation began to form in his head, and in the evening he phoned Pavel the Czechoslovakian, a plumber for whom he did odd jobs, to ask his advice. Some days late, they drove by the house before going for a beer at a nearby hotel.

'A good buy, excellent location,' the plumber said in the pub. 'Five minutes to Central Station, fifteen to the City Hall.'

'Terrible condition inside,' Alfonso said.

'Think of the price.' Pavel signalled the barmaid for another round.

Alfonso's friend Nick recommended a solicitor. The solicitor suggested St George Building Society as the lender, and the deposit was paid and the contracts signed. Five weeks later there was a thick envelope in his letterbox, which he slit open in the kitchen with the breadknife. It contained the settlement papers, dated July 10, 1968. The key to the house was at the agent's city office.

That evening, he sang in the shower. In between grilling veal chops and frying chips and capsicums, he held a glass of wine in one hand and the spatula in the other and pretended that he was dancing with a beautiful woman.

As the evening advanced, the current of emotions filling the room was disrupted by a kind of sadness at the thought of leaving Woolloomooloo. While doing the dishes, he looked out the kitchen window. The neglected lot, the cemetery of bottles, and the playground of birds and stray cats lay silent. The windows of surrounding houses were dark, their dormant chimneys dim silhouettes against the pale sky.

This had been his vista, except for three months spent at Raul's house, during his six years in Australia. The vista he had shared with passing sailors, with providers of instant love, with failed men sleeping in doorways, for whom he felt both sympathy and contempt at the urine puddles and flattened cardboard they left behind in the morning. And with the big, handsome cat with the shiny black coat and amazing golden eyes, walking along the parapet of the neighbour's roof every Sunday between three and four in the afternoon. Sometimes he would stop and look intently as Alfonso folded the washing or cleaned the place, but not always. Mostly he would go on for another ten metres, turn left and re-emerge minutes later on the ground in the empty lot, glance again at Alfonso, and disappear in the overgrowth. All gestures of friendship had been ignored. Only once he seemed to have prickled his ears when Alfonso remarked that they were both creatures of habit.

The following day he went from work to the agent's office, collected the key, and hurried to the house. As he opened the front door a putrid smell rushed out at him. He felt sick halfway to the back of the house, and he vomited in the backyard.

He remembered that during the brief inspection, the real estate agent had attributed the bad smell, which he called 'stuffiness,' to the fact that the place been closed up for a long time. Ten minutes later, his stomach settled a little and he went back inside, now with a handkerchief to his mouth and nose, and opened the upstairs windows.

On the way back to the bed-sitter, he reflected how less than an hour ago he had arrived with the key in his clenched hand and his heart filled with joy. Now the reek of rotting seafood and cabbage, and something else he couldn't place, followed him like a swarm of hungry flies.

Once home, he found no pleasure in his after-work shower or in cooking his dinner. The wine tasted like vinegar. All the excitement of the previous day had been replaced by a growing suspicion that he had made a mistake in buying the house, which had all the basics, but would require lots of time and money to fix. And although he had contributed sixty-five percent, owing money to the bank worried him.

Later in a dream, a bluish fog with the unidentified fetid smell of the house entered his room and slowly permeated his cupboards and clothes. Not even the foil-wrapped sandwiches for work and the coffee thermos were spared.

He returned the next afternoon with a mask, and every afternoon after that. A week later, the backyard was a mountain of mangy floor coverings and rotting kitchen cupboards.

He took Saturday off work and together with Jesus, the driver from Rubbish Removals, cleared the site. They had tied the last pieces of carpet over the third and final load when the brothers Ramirez stopped by on their way from work. They had brought cold beer and they all stood in the just-cleared backyard, drinking. When one of the brothers commented on the strange lingering odour inside the house, Jesus said it was the smell of death. As if required to provide supporting evidence, he mentioned he had first migrated from Spain to Venezuela, describing in minute detail his work as a handyman in the crematorium of Cementerio Metropolitano, in Caracas, which included pulling out the red button to activate the circular saw that sliced the coffin in half, and pushing in the dark green button that ignited the oven burners.

During the second week, Alfonso gave two coats of white paint to the front bedroom. And from the Salvation Army store in Tempe he bought a washing machine, a table, four chairs, and a bed with a carved headboard in need of a good sanding and coat of varnish.

Noon Sunday, Pavel came to the bed-sitter and helped Alfonso carry his suitcase, tools, and several boxes of assorted stuff to the truck. They were already in the driver's cab when Alfonso felt he had forgotten something, and returned.

In the room, he gazed about. He had left nothing behind. He had returned, he realised, to say goodbye to all the hopes and hardships of the past six years.

The four walls he had washed and painted twice as a gesture of friendship would have captured, as a mirror would, his frustration at trying to sew on a button, or trying not to scorch a new shirt; his clumsy attempts at cooking dinner with half of the ingredients missing until he trained himself to write a shopping list before going shopping; his relentless learning and re-learning of English words; his chores of washing, cleaning, daily bed-making, and weekly changing of the bed sheets.

These same walls would have recorded his loneliness in daytime and sadness always at night. The narrow wardrobe, the Triumph stove, the couch, two wooden chairs, and the aluminium table with the green Formica top would have watched his character crossing from youth to man, although he could not identify the exact turning point. Perhaps the pieces came together like a jigsaw. He remembered feeling proud of doing his job well, of having the first thousand-dollar balance stamped in his ANZ Bank savings book. Above all, he had been deeply thankful for having escaped poverty, for being in control of his life, and for how good a life he had.

And there was the vague beginning, and understanding, of the forming of his two selves—one made of past memories, the other of new dreams. Dreams had been good companions in the village and they remained so in Australia. Three of them had crystallised into purpose: the satisfactory command of the English language, the owning of a house, and the companionship of a woman. The first two were going well, he thought.

He took one last look out the small window above the granite sink, and returned to the truck where an impatient Pavel wanted to know what kept him so long.

In the afternoon, he mopped the floors with disinfectant and cleaned the stove, the fridge, and a timber wardrobe, the three items he had been able to salvage.

He dined on bread and cheese and drank half a bottle of wine, sitting on the dilapidated verandah floor, his back against the wall. On the footpath in front of the house, there was a tree the same height as the verandah. It had thin branches and sickly leaves. Its head had been repeatedly lopped off as it reached the electrical wires, and it had lost the will to grow. He would try to restore its confidence by removing the weeds at its base and supplying it with water and fertiliser.

From somewhere in the neighbourhood came the sound of a baby crying, a door banging, a bird calling. The city was only pretending to be quiet in the dark. He became aware of the buzz of a plane, its lights blinking through the night sky. Beyond the plane was the universe itself, nicely lit by uncountable stars for which, like his feelings, he had no names.

Now and then a silhouette appeared briefly in the lighted windows across the road. Someone undressed. After the last light went out, he went inside and climbed into bed. He thought that the mattress was much softer than the vinyl sofa bed of the bed-sitter. Then he thought of the people who had lived in the house and the people who had slept on his new bed. How many beds had he slept in? The answer: seven. Bright shadows slid across the ceiling each time a car drove by on the street below, and he wondered where he could get some curtains.

In the morning he woke from a dream that he could not remember, but the feeling of excitement was the same as the one he had felt as a boy of eight when, from outside the kitchen door, he had once heard Sacundino, an old friend of his father, promising his mother to make the boy his apprentice on his twelfth birthday. Now in his mind there were clear images of Sacundino, a carpenter in his early sixties, small, thin, with a lined face and snow white hair. He began collecting misfortunes the hour his mother died giving birth to him. At thirteen he lost his right eye, and at seventeen, a badly set broken leg resulted in a limp. Other hardships included a botched hernia operation, stomach ulcers, and rheumatism, yet he handled it all with grace, and his actions remained noble.

Alfonso had been his apprentice for seven years. When they were not at their homes for spring sowing and summer harvesting, they went around the surrounding villages making or repairing ploughs, cupboards, and the occasional bed, wardrobe, or carved dining room table and chairs. They worked for their meals and a very small wage. It was that or nothing. Their most reliable work was making coffins, from humble pine to elaborate chestnut, until a returned migrant from Panama opened a joinery, where the machines worked day and night like death itself.

One night in late July, Alfonso was awakened by the panes of the French doors rattling in their frames. It had rained during the day and the roof leaked in every room and continued leaking long after the rain stopped. He moved his bed to the front room downstairs and rang the plumber.

'Water trapped by the plaster ceilings,' Pavel said on the telephone.

'New roof and new ceilings,' he added later in the week as he came down the ladder from a quick inspection of the attic.

Alfonso brought out a bottle of wine and two glasses. They

sat at the kitchen table. Pavel said that the plaster ceilings were held up by timber rivets and in pulling them down, you also pulled down a hundred years of accumulated black dust, which would billow out of the doors and windows like smoke from a house on fire. 'You too will run out for fresh air. Expect to cough nasty stuff for weeks.'

The plumber did not lie.

Within two months, his cash reserves were gone. But the house had a new, galvanised iron roof and plaster ceilings, and the double bed again in the newly painted front room upstairs. During a batch of wet weather, he used the time off work to chip away at the old, greasy paint from the kitchen walls, aware of the rain tapping away like an endless lullaby.

The letter from Town Hall came on a Friday. The neighbour on his right, it said, had complained of dust and hammering, and the one on his left demanded compensation for cracks on their common wall. Alfonso had exchanged nods with one, never met the other. He was preoccupied the whole weekend. He felt that, as his mother used to say, no good bread would come out of this dough, and he sought advice from his supervisor at work.

'They got you by the balls,' the supervisor said, still looking at the council's letter.

'I haven't done anything wrong.'

'Don't worry,' said the supervisor, sensing Alfonso's uneasiness. 'I'll talk to someone in the office.'

Alfonso thanked him.

Later the same afternoon, the supervisor informed him to go easy on the noise and be ready to fork out $200 for a structural engineer's certificate.

The council meeting took place on a Monday morning in Alfonso's front room. The two neighbours, Alfonso, and the building inspector stood in a circle. The building inspector, a tall man with a kind face, thinning hair, and a generous belly, spoke with a file under his arm and a briefcase between his legs. He addressed one neighbour by telling Alfonso to work quietly and to work only during the permitted hours. He said to the other that the wall's cracks had been caused by poor foundations. He gave each of them a letter confirming the council's view and their rights as taxpayers to accept or reject it.

The neighbours left.

'May I look around?' asked the senior building inspector.

'Yes, of course,' said Alfonso.

'What are you trying to do with the place?' he asked as they walked up the stairs.

'Clean it up. Make it liveable.'

'No outside extensions?'

'No.'

In the backyard, the inspector walked into the laundry shed, lifted the lid off the old copper boiler, and looked in. He mentioned the need for new wiring and plumbing, as well as rising damp and the difficulty of fixing it. He then walked to the tall, narrow brick structure at the end of the yard, opened the rusty door, and shook his head. 'This spiders' paradise was once the loo,' he said. 'Used to be a bucket under the seat that the council changed every week. Did you know that?'

Alfonso didn't know.

Then he said, 'Careful with the bricks. They will be worth a dollar each soon.'

'Why?' Alfonso asked.

'Made by convicts. They baked them in the sun.'

In the kitchen, he stood his briefcase on the old woodstove. He asked Alfonso for a screwdriver and carefully scraped the paint until he found a brick with the imprint of a heart. 'That's the work-gang's trademark,' he said.

Alfonso moved closer to look at the convict-made bricks, a subject new to him, and made a mental note for his next visited to the public library.

Before he left, the inspector gave Alfonso his business card and wished him luck.

Alfonso closed the front door, went to the kitchen, and had salami and bread for lunch. Afterwards, he fitted his scotch hammer with new teeth and chipped at the paint on the hallway. He thought of the meeting, of the hostility in the air. One neighbour had only looked at the dusty floor; the other had had an expression on his face that contained many things, none of them good. Then he thought of how in the village, neighbours talked to one another, shared the news, celebrated special occasions, remedied a shortfall of cooking oil, sugar, even a decent pair of trousers or a shirt to dress up a corpse laid out for the viewing.

But then, he thought, he was not qualified to judge these two men, despite their unfriendliness. Even though he had been in Australia for six years, he had a limited understanding of the country's customs and values. His existence had been confined to the bed-sitter and now to the house. He was protected by human absence. Like a recluse living on an island, he crossed a bridge to go to work, shop, and return. His Saturday night outings to the Spanish or Italian or German clubs took place on Australian soil, but his companions were migrants like himself, their language Spanish, the topic women. And he thought of his days in the village and the Sunday trips to a nearby village or town where a dance might be. Perhaps it was he, Alfonso, who failed to engage with the world around him because, in many ways, he still lived in his past.

Later in the afternoon, Alfonso was using a steamer to remove ancient wallpaper when Pavel knocked at the front door.

'You read my thoughts,' Alfonso said, pointing at the two bottles of beer in the plumber's hand.

Pavel poured the beer into coffee mugs. Alfonso splashed water on his face and the back of his neck at the kitchen sink.

'You have no water pressure because the old iron pipes are blocked with rust,' said Pavel, pointing at the brown, thread-like stream coming out of the tap.

'You already told me that they would have to be replaced with copper ones,' Alfonso said.

'There is another problem.'

'Is that why you're here?'

'Mate, it's your luck. According to the Water Board, the back lane's main is ancient and there is no guarantee of supply. And the new main is at the front of the house, on the other side of the road.'

'You mean …'

'Yes. The road will have to be cut to lay the new pipe. And there is a fee for a Main Roads' permit and a map showing where the gas and phone lines are.'

Alfonso opened the other bottle of beer.

A couple of days after the conversation with Pavel, Alfonso discovered that termites had all but eaten the doorframe of the third bedroom. Further inspection confirmed that the floor joists, architraves, and skirting boards throughout the house had been affected.

'How many bad things can happen to me?' he asked himself. He flung the screwdriver into the toolbox and made his way to the backyard. Resting his hands on the palings of the back fence, he gazed at the gold sunset behind the houses, then at the children playing cricket down the lane. He became conscious of two black birds looking solemnly at him from their perch on a power line and went indoors and poured himself a glass of wine. He sat at the bottom of the stairs and watched the dark stealing in through the window.

It may have been after the second or third drink that he remembered old Sacundino's words: 'Luck is your life's companion. Sometimes she's generous. Sometimes she's cruel. But she never takes everything away from you.' And it was true. Despite the calamities that had followed one another, the house had a new roof and solid walls made of bricks that were worth a dollar each, according to the council's inspector.

The room filled with shadows. He thought he heard termites dining on the scanty remains of his timbers. Then he thought he heard Sacundino's old man's voice, muffled by distance, telling him to stop tormenting himself. So he went to bed and thought about the fishing season and his regular fishing companions: Amador, now dead, and Fernando, not heard from since he went to France well before Alfonso came to Australia. And he could hear the sound of the stream and see the colours on the trout's back.

Each morning at six, Alfonso left for work and returned at five in the afternoon. He took his shoes off and changed clothes in the laundry. He poured a glass of wine, peeled the potatoes standing at the sink, put them on to boil with the carrots, placed the meat on the grill, and sat down at the kitchen table. While waiting, he leafed through a *House and Garden* magazine he had borrowed from the library, stopping now and then to read or gaze at the pictures.

After dinner, he cleared the table, fought a brief temptation to leave the dishes in the sink, and resumed work on whichever endless task of renovation he was currently engaged in. At ten o'clock, he took a shower, made the sandwiches for the following day, and went to bed.

He did not go out on weekends. He ordered materials as money became available, learned new skills, and bartered old ones with the bricklayer, the plasterers, and the electrician. He worked every spare hour, with the radio for company, often imagining that one day he would meet a beautiful woman who would live there with him and all would be perfect. No more eating and sleeping alone.

Late one evening, just as he was going upstairs to bed, he heard something scratching against the back door. Instead of some lost woman looking for a friend, or some dusky angel wanting a bed, in the light of the doorway he saw the big, handsome cat with the shiny black coat and astonishing golden eyes. It seemed to be injured. Alfonso fetched a bowl of milk and placed it outside the door. The cat straightened up a little, eagerly lapped the milk, and slowly walked away before Alfonso had a chance to say how happy he was to see him again and to apologise for leaving the bed-sitter without saying goodbye.

Alfonso was not surprised to see the cat. He knew that cats found their way home over long distances. A memory came back to him of a young cat named Marela, the yellow one, his mother had given to her sister who lived some eight kilometres away. To their astonishment, Marela was back three weeks later (she lapped all the milk available and slept for two days). In this case, the distance was only a fifth of that. But there had not been closeness between them. Curiosity certainly—or perhaps a routine that reminded them both it was Saturday. The new encounter was just a coincidence, Alfonso thought, as he took the bowl to the sink to wash.

The cat returned a few days later. Alfonso had left the door ajar and a bowl of leftovers nearby. When the cat didn't come inside, Alfonso took the food bowl outside. The cat did not eat until Alfonso moved away.

'Perhaps you have acquired bad table manners,' Alfonso said. 'I understand. I, too, have been eating by myself for a long time. Do you mind if I call you Guapo?'

The ritual continued for a few weeks. Then, one day Guapo entered the house and wandered into every room with the familiar curiosity of an old resident returning. Inspection completed, he sat on an old wrought iron chair Alfonso used for the radio or to take a short rest while working, and he watched Alfonso erect the brick piers for the new floor joist.

Guapo visited two, sometimes three times a week and always at night. He would eat only outside the back door, and alone. Often, after a brief sniff at the food, he would refuse to eat at all.

'You are a spoiled cat,' Alfonso said to him one time, pointing to the pork chop rinds and vegetables untouched on the blue-rimmed, white porcelain plate. 'Soon you will demand roasted pigeons as if you were a cat of ancient Egypt. There, the *Reader's Digest* says, cats were treated like kings. But you are in Australia! You should be grateful. Just imagine if you were born where I was. Your first problem would be the colour of your coat. The sight of a black cat with intense yellow eyes, especially in the morning, would be almost as bad as seeing a woman picking herbs in the moonlight. And you would have to scrounge most of your food. Yes, you can see in the dark, but mice are no fools. You would spend many restless nights with an empty stomach, and long days stalking sparrows instead of snoozing in the sun.'

The cat stood up, then lay down again.

'You would think me a savage if I were to describe to you the various ways I have disposed of unwanted kittens. Perhaps I was, and I'm not proud of what I did, but it was a task for the boys, part of growing up. And the cats themselves were partly to blame. They were valuable members of every household, entrusted with the safekeeping of the granary. But they bred too often, breaking the basic rule that regulates the proportion of cats to mice: too many mice make cats fat and lazy, too few mice and the cats go hungry. In any case, they were better off than your comrades in other countries where they end up on the menu along with snakes, turtles, and dogs. But I'll say no more. I don't want to give you nightmares.'

Soon, Alfonso knew that mackerel, sardine, and chicken liver were Guapo's preferred foods. He also concluded reluctantly that in Guapo's heart, there was limited space for him. But all was forgiven the moment he announced his arrival with meows and proceeded to rub himself against Alfonso's legs. They would go to the kitchen together and fix his dinner. The meal over, Guapo would return to where Alfonso was working, sit on his chair, now cushioned with an old towel, and wash himself thoroughly. He napped or followed Alfonso around, watching him re-rope and reglaze sash windows, or sand, varnish, and rehang doors. Thus they went from room to room, and from summer to winter and round to summer again.

Now and then, Alfonso felt a little envious of the cat's night prowls. Not that Guapo bragged or boasted of anything; sometimes he just looked pleased with himself.

Alfonso was also concerned for the cat's well being when he arrived smeared with blood. Once he had an ear almost ripped off and was reluctant to let Alfonso clean the wound. 'You take it easy for a while,' Alfonso said when the cat finished a good ration of steamed chicken giblets and joined him in the upstairs room, where he was affixing a ceiling rose. Guapo stopped washing himself and twitched his tail as if in agreement.

'About the fight,' Alfonso asked in a while, 'was she good-looking?'

By then Guapo was lying on his belly, eyes closed, paws folded neatly beneath him, and Alfonso knew that conversation was over for the night.

Late one night, while dismantling the living room fireplace for cleaning and resetting, he came across a bundle of newspapers tucked up the chimney. He pulled them out, and Guapo, until then dozing in his usual place, meowed loudly and ran away.

Alfonso headed for the backyard to see what Guapo was up to, but there was no sign of him. Still wondering about the cat's behaviour, he re-entered the house, sat on the metal toolbox, and placed the bundle of papers on his knees. The outermost sheet was dirty and unreadable, the inner ones yellowed but in readable condition. There were full pages and small cuttings. The thrust was about a murder, apparently unsolved. Alfonso was curious, but he was tired and it was approaching midnight.

His friend Mauricio called early the next morning with the trailer, and they cleared the site of the fireplace rubbish, including the newspaper cuttings.

Days later at work, Alfonso mentioned to Nick the cat's sudden departure.

'Cats always know what they want,' Nick replied. 'But don't think he is gone for good.'

Alfonso wanted to believe his colleague. He missed Guapo, his meows and head-butts, his conversation. Heavy silence sat on the wrought iron chair in his absence. Perhaps I bored him, Alfonso thought, with my reprimands for being so fussy with food, and my improper questions of what he saw in the bedrooms from the roofs and window sills, what he knew of women and other men's skills in the business of seduction.

Alfonso had been selfish, always dealing with his own preoccupations, not even having the decency to enquire about Guapo's family, his friends, his happiness. If Guapo ever came back, Alfonso promised himself he would be a considerate friend.

About a month after Guapo's departure, Alfonso was in the laundry soaking his work clothes when he first heard the voice.

'I like the new living room very much. The two windows at each end make it bright and spacious … lovely. I can already imagine the sun on the new polished floorboards in the early morning and late afternoon. But don't touch the fireplace.'

It was a woman's voice, distant and melancholy, and she spoke in English. For a moment, he thought it came from the copper boiler, and he even lifted the lid. Then he thought it came from outside, so he looked out the window before returning to the washing. He was disturbed by the voice and also had a suspicion that someone was reading his thoughts. Only a month earlier he had converted the small living room and dining room into a big room by removing the wall between them, and now he was thinking that without the fireplace, the room would look wider.

I am imagining things, he said to himself, and resumed the washing. But later in the day, he thought that something was not right. There had been too many unusual happenings, and he was troubled, although he did not know why.

One evening some weeks later, he was at the kitchen table putting together an order for plaster cornices when she spoke again. She complimented him on the restored French doors and said she was looking forward to seeing the verandah's rusted ironwork brought back to life. Then she said the ceiling plasterwork mould and cornices should be replicas of the originals. She seemed to be aware of his thinking when she added, 'Even though the plain ones are cheaper, they will change the character of the house. Same goes for the architraves and skirting boards.'

He thought the voice came from the shadows outside the half-open kitchen door, so he pushed away the papers with the calculations, darted to the living room, and switched on the ceiling light. He checked every room upstairs. It was all as it should be, but afterwards, he would recall that the French doors to the verandah were open and that there was a faint scent of mimosa in the room.

Her arrivals and departures were as silent as the shadow of a sundial. While in the house, she stood at the top of the stairs or in doorways or in a corner of the room, away from the light of the naked bulb and away from him. She spoke softly and moved swiftly. She had no shape; often she was silent, yet Alfonso was aware of her presence. At other times, opinions were murmured into his thoughts from far away: 'It would be sacrilege to replace the rotten window frame with an aluminium one … maybe rebuild the bathroom and laundry at the back … it would be nice to have a shower and toilet upstairs…'

'There is no room upstairs for a bathroom,' he said, disturbed by the sound of his own voice.

'Partition the middle room. Women don't like to go too far from their beds. And the days of the chamber pot are over, you know.'

'I will never finish if I keep listening to you!'

'Yes, but are you really in such a hurry?'

In addition to partitioning the middle room for a shower and toilet, she suggested he convert the remaining space into a walk-in wardrobe and linen press. But it was when she mentioned the need for a broom cupboard that he got really angry and told her to go to hell. She laughed out loud. It was the first time he'd heard her laugh.

There was no argument as to the new kitchen. He had widened the window to capture extra light, winter sun, and a wider view of the neighbour's two tall trees with leaves that shivered even in the absence of wind. He had removed layers of grease and paint from the walls before cement-rendering them. For the floor, he chose terracotta tiles that complemented the marble bench top with black, green, and red veins. He bought recycled English oak and Western red cedar for the cupboards, and he carved flowers in the panels. He whittled fish-shaped handles for the doors and drawers from driftwood picked up at Bronte Beach.

One evening, past ten o'clock, he had finished mounting the telephone on the wall, the last item on his list, when he thought he heard the bedroom floorboards creak. Half expecting her, he switched on the range hood light and sat down in the semi-darkness with a glass of wine. He liked what he saw and was a little disappointed when she didn't comment. Then he reasoned that her interest in the kitchen had always been minimal.

Chapter 2

The much-anticipated event, that the electrician called a house-warming party, took place on Sunday July 10, 1971—two years, eleven months, and one week from the day he moved in. The busy week leading up to it had been made worse by the territorial war between Roy, the carpet layer, and Leon, the floor sander. It was dinnertime on Saturday when Alfonso finally cleaned and put away the paintbrushes.

He rose at daybreak on Sunday, made coffee, and sipped it while washing the plates, knives, and forks he had bought at St Vincent de Paul's earlier in the week. He then cleaned the house and the backyard. When the sun broke through the clouds, he took it as an omen for a perfect winter day, his anxiety softening a little.

The brothers Ramirez came at twelve, bringing with them trestles and planks to set up a long table in the yard. Mauricio was next, with a grill and a barbecue plate, then Pavel, with beer and bags of ice. Claire, Pavel's fiancée, and a friend, came soon after that. The friend's name was Nancy. She was about Alfonso's age and height and wore a cream dress and brown leather sandals. Her face was thin, her skin pale-white. She had a lovely mouth and faded-blue eyes.

By one o'clock, all the guests—ten men and seven women—had arrived. The laundry had become a bar, and the kitchen counter and table disappeared under a colourful array of meats, salads and pastries. Blue smoke from the fire, blended with the aromas of saffron and garlic and olive oil, wafted through the house, displacing the scent of floor polish and fresh paint. Food, wine, and laughter mingled with music from a portable record player. Pedro, the blacksmith, won the meat-eating competition with seven

T-bone steaks. Raul came in second with six pork chops.

By the time the afternoon shadows darkened the yard, the women had moved to the living room for coffee. Alfonso apologised for the lack of proper liqueur glasses as he poured anisette into their coffee cups. The card players in the kitchen requested brandy. In the backyard, another group entertained themselves with coarse jokes and icy beers from the laundry tub.

As evening approached, lights came on up and down the back lane. Pedro rekindled the barbeque, and the Ramirez brothers arranged chicken wings on a tray with mushrooms and rump steak.

It was midnight when Alfonso took the last cups and glasses to the sink, put out the lights, and got into bed. He savoured the compliments.

'The polished hardwood floor in the living room is lovely.'

'Where did you get the federation plaster cornice?'

'Who designed your bathrooms?'

'Who planned your kitchen?'

He thought of Nancy's brown hair shining in the sunlight, Nancy carrying a bowl of salad, Nancy in the kitchen, a plate in one hand, a dishcloth in the other. Though he was exhausted, he did not fall asleep until three in the morning.

She had been the first to leave.

'Thank you for your help,' he said as he walked her to the car.

'That's OK. I had a good time, too.' She waved as she drove away, and he waved back.

Her soft voice was still with him in the morning. The way she moved and spoke and laughed was vaguely familiar, but he couldn't say how or why. She was often in his thoughts throughout the week, and on Saturday he called Pavel.

'Claire and I were just talking of you,' Pavel said. 'Nancy

has been asking questions.'

'What about?'

'She is keen.'

'Well…'

'It will cost you.'

'How much?'

'Lunch.'

'Agreed.'

On Sunday, two weeks later, the four of them went to Manly for lunch. It was a warm August day with bright sunshine. Sailboats crisscrossed the harbour. Claire drove with Pavel beside her. Nancy and Alfonso sat in the back. Nancy was dressed in sandals, light-coloured shorts, and a pale green blouse.

'You are very quiet, Pavel,' Alfonso said.

He was trying to divert his thoughts from the effects of Nancy's scent and proximity.

'I have a headache,' he said.

'He has a hangover,' Claire said and smiled.

'Were you out late last night?' Nancy asked him.

'Drinking with his building mates,' Claire said.

Pavel shook his head.

Claire parked the white Volkswagen at the wharf, and they walked to the beach side. They chose a seafood café and a table on the terrace with a view of the sand, the sun sparkling on the water, and shrieking seagulls. The waiter suggested a platter of grilled fish with salad. They drank beer and white wine. Alfonso paid, happily.

Outside the café, Claire suggested they go for a walk on the beach. Pavel nodded. But then he said that he was in no mood for walking, and he would wait for them at the hotel down the road. Claire sighed, stared at him for a moment and then at the sea.

The three walked mostly in silence along the water's edge to the end of the beach and back. Now and then Claire picked up a shell. Dead souls, she called them. They drove back in the late afternoon. Nancy spoke about her coming trip to England to attend a cousin's wedding. Alfonso thought that she was making conversation to ease the silence hanging heavily between Claire and Pavel. That night in bed, he recalled the gentle music of the ocean, Nancy's perfect legs, and glimpses of her breast as she bent down to select a shell for her friend.

Alfonso and Nancy met a fortnight later, a Sunday afternoon, in the foyer of the Century Cinema in George Street to see *Willy Wonka & the Chocolate Factory*. Her perfume was the same as the one she wore for their trip to Manly with Pavel and Claire. He thought she was very quiet during intermission, commenting only that the film would appeal to both adults and children. Nor did she say much on the way to her red Morris Minor parked on Sussex Street, or as she drove to his place. And she didn't accept his invitation to come into the house.

'I've been out on Friday and Saturday. I'm worn out,' she said. Then she leaned over, and for a tiny moment, her lips touched the side of his face, leaving an intense warmth that he clung to for the rest of the evening.

A week or so passed before she phoned.

'Did you like the film?' she asked.

'Very much.'

'Do you go to the cinema a lot?'

'Not as much I would like to.'

'Why not?'

'I don't like to go by myself.'

'We can fix that.'

She had seen many films, she said. 'Best place for dreaming and staying cool in summer,' she added.

He asked when they could meet again.

'Would you like to go for a long drive?' she asked.

'Yes,' he answered.

They settled the date. He put the receiver back on the hook and danced around the kitchen table.

Walking home from work the next day, he passed by the local pre-school playgroup, which he had barely noticed before, and stopped. It was already late in the afternoon and there were no children about, yet he imagined them at play and the idea that he liked children came to him suddenly. Then he thought about Nancy as he started again for Charles Street.

Nancy arrived at Alfonso's house at eight o'clock Sunday morning carrying a cardboard box containing a red pot.

'Dinner,' she said, 'ready for the stove when we come back.' Alfonso wanted to ask her what they'd be eating. Then he wanted to tell her she looked good in her jeans and white blouse. Instead, he offered her a cup of coffee.

Nancy's Morris Minor was parked in front of the house. She turned the ignition key. 'We are on our way,' she said. The city had the cool, clean, morning smell. The business houses and car yards along Parramatta Road were not yet open. The radio had predicted storms in the afternoon, but Alfonso gazed at a cloudless sky.

'Typical September,' Nancy said. 'I'd like to know more about you,' she added a while later.

'What would you like to know?' He glanced at her profile and at her long fingers curved gently around the steering wheel. Then he looked out the window and saw 'Welcome to Ashfield' written in flowers on the side of the road.

'Everything, but you can start by telling me how long you've been in Australia?'

'Nine years.'

'Do you like it here?'

'I do.'

'And how about the people?'

'Australians?'

'Yes, do you like Australians?'

'Some of them regard immigrants with curiosity, some with mistrust. A man at work says the smell of garlic and olive oil is spreading like a plague. Another says we're a threat to the Australian way of life. But I have no reason to complain.'

'Your English is good. Where did you learn it?'

'I went to language classes for two years. I read and listen to the radio.'

'And you work in the building industry?'

'Yes. I am a form worker.'

'I'm not sure I know what that means.'

'I'm a carpenter. The company I work for specialises in building office blocks. I make timber structures that are later filled with steel and concrete.'

'You don't sound enthusiastic about it.'

'The pay is good and it requires no thinking, only precise measuring and cutting. 'Measure twice and cut once,' as an old friend used to say. But I'm a carpenter of another kind. A cabinet maker, I think they call it in Australia.'

'Have you tried finding other jobs?'

'A friend and I considered opening a small workshop and making handmade furniture, but then I bought the house and became preoccupied with the renovations and needed the safety of a weekly income to pay for them, so I stayed where I was.'

'You've done a good job renovating the house.'

'Thank you. Friends helped.'

They were silent.

'And you?' he asked.

'I'm just a typical girl from the suburbs. After school, I got a job with ANZ Bank, and now I'm with the NRMA. My mother died when I was fourteen, and my father teaches maths at Dulwich High School. I'm twenty-eight, and I have a younger brother. Do you have family?'

'A mother and a brother. My father died in the Civil War.'

'Terrible. Do you remember him?'

'Not clearly.'

Alfonso had a single vivid image of a faded photograph in his mother's bedroom. There was also the collective memory of village children waiting for their fathers every afternoon by the side of the road. Some fathers returned. Some children laughed, and others cried and waited until after dark, but he did not tell her that.

Outside the car window, the landscape of car yards, factories, and petrol stations gave way to market gardens and open country. An hour into their journey, Nancy left the highway for a smaller road that curled up and down hills covered with bushes and gum trees. They stopped for several minutes at a clearing by the side of the road. Nancy picked wildflowers, and Alfonso walked a short distance to urinate. Leaves swished high above him. There were no bird sounds in the trees. Nearby, a brown lizard watched him intently.

Nancy offered him the flowers to smell before placing them in the backseat of the car. He thought the colours of the flowers in Australia were less vivid than those in his old village, and he was surprised he could not name a single native Australian shrub or flower.

When they were back on the road, he said, 'The eucalyptus reminds me of home. We call them the plague from Australia.'

'Why is that?' she asked.

'They take over.'

Nancy laughed. 'How did eucalyptus get there?'

'From Italy. Mussolini imported them to drain the swamps.'

'That's some story. Where did you hear it?'

'In the village.'

'What else reminds you of home?'

'Well, the crows always make me think of home.'

'Another plague from Australia?' She glanced at him with a smile.

'No. Crows are associated with death.'

'Do you believe in those superstitions?'

'I don't know. I grew up with them.'

They rode in silence, and arrived at the Jenolan Caves close to noon. In the car park, Nancy stretched her arms and legs. Alfonso stood by, watching the sun being swallowed by a huge mountain of dark clouds.

In the peaceful belly of the caves, people moved slowly, whispering or in silence. He and Nancy walked side by side; Alfonso's mouth was half open, his eyes focused on the stalactites hanging from the roof and slim stalagmites rising from the floor. Alabaster columns, delightful shawls, drops of water trickling down a wall, leaving sheets of crystal behind. Lovely, he thought.

Afterwards, they walked to the café adjoining the souvenir shop, crowded with tourists like themselves. Nancy ordered ham and chicken sandwiches and tea from the woman behind the counter, and Alfonso paid for them. Sitting opposite one another at a small red-topped table, he wanted to tell her that in the caves he felt small and insignificant, like when he looked at stars at night. He also wanted to say that he liked her, that even tea tasted good in her company, but the words did not come to his lips.

Fat drops of rain fell as they left the café, and thunder rumbled above them, so they took refuge in the souvenir shop. Half an hour later, they braved the rain and ran to the car. They travelled slowly on the road, which was half-obscured under the sheets of rain. The windscreen wipers swiped up and down with a noisy clatter. Now and then, Nancy glanced at Alfonso. On one occasion, she patted his knee. He felt strangely content.

'There was a serious rainstorm the other time I travelled on this road,' Alfonso said, after the rain had eased a little and they could hear each another.

'Really? Tell me more—what happened?'

'It's a long story.'

'We have time. Look at the creeping traffic in front of us.'

'It's not a pleasant story.'

'OK. I'd like to hear it all the same.'

'I don't know how to begin.'

'I'll help you get started. I guess you were in a car, right?'

'Yes.'

'Were you driving alone?'

'No. I was with Raul and Salvador.'

'Who are they?'

'You met Raul at the barbecue. He's short and square, with a moustache.'

'And his wife has tiny eyes?'

'That's him.'

'OK. So you were driving with Raul and Salvador. Where were you going?'

'We came to buy two sheep.'

'Sheep!' She frowned.'

Alfonso paused for a long moment. 'As I said, we came to buy two sheep. It was another of Raul's ideas for getting a cheap supply of meat. We were already purchasing a forty-four-gallon drum of red wine from Griffith every other month, which provided us with fun on bottling day and much cheap wine.

'One Sunday, Salvador called for me at seven, and we drove to Raul's house in Surry Hills. It was like this morning: clear sky and light traffic. Salvador drove. Raul navigated, using a street directory and a map drawn by his friend Theo Marinopoulos. I sat in the back of the big Valiant. We were excited; we had travelled from the other side of the world but had not once gone this far from our suburbs.

'We reached Parramatta just before eleven. As we left the business district, Raul told us we had one hour to go. Soon, we saw farmhouses and fields. Half an hour later, we were lost, so we drove back and asked directions at the petrol station. The man said, "Turn right after the bridge, turn left before the train crossing, and keep going for about a mile."

'We followed his instructions and got lost again. Salvador blamed Raul and his map. We didn't talk for a while. Then Raul said that deficient road signs and the Australian way of driving on the left confused him. Salvador laughed loudly, the back of Raul's neck reddened above the collar of his blue shirt, and I got worried. He has a nasty temper. I also knew that Salvador—people call him "the gypsy" because of his coal-black hair and olive skin—Salvador would not retreat from a fight. He always carried a knife with him.

'The mood in the car was tense, so I suggested that we stop for a bite to eat and a glass of wine. We parked on high ground, several metres from the road, and sat in the shade of a eucalyptus tree with a view of a farmhouse in a valley.

There were big brown ants on the ground, and kookaburras in the trees, but they didn't distract us from the lunch Raul's wife had packed for us—some bread and chicken legs, a big lump of Edam cheese, and three bottles of wine.

'We pulled back onto the road calmer, but running out of hope that we'd find the place. Twenty minutes later, we saw the ram's horns on the letterbox, which was the sign we had been searching for the last two hours.

'I can still see Raul rubbing his hands together as he left the car to open the property's gate.

'The farmer said, "You're late, I have other things to do than wait all day for you." He took us to a paddock behind a shed and said "Take your pick and be done with it."

'We stood around a small enclosure looking at thirty or so sheep staring back at us with vacant expressions. Salvador volunteered to do the selecting, but he took his time poking and prodding before choosing the two he liked best.

'Raul told the farmer to kill them for us, but the farmer said "Twenty bucks a head, as is. Take them or leave them."'

Alfonso paused in his story.

'And you took them?' prompted Nancy.

'We did. The farmer put the notes in his pocket, told us to make sure we shut the gate, and started for the main house.'

'And then?'

'We tied their legs and put them in the boot of the Valiant, which was too small. The door could not latch and had to be secured with a rope.'

'And you drove away, pleased with yourselves, I imagine.'

'We were. Salvador played one of his tapes. I passed the wine bottle, and Raul said he was looking forward to the skinning and butchering of our bounty. In all the excitement, we didn't notice that the sky had gone dark until the wind and rain suddenly started hammering the car. Before long, we were merely crawling along, very much like we are now. The car started shuddering, and Salvador said the engine was no good in the wet. A while later, we noticed that people were staring at us, some even blowing their horns. Raul told Salvador not to take any notice of the people, just drive. It was only when the tape finished playing and the rain eased that we heard the sheep bleating in the boot. It was rather unpleasant.'

'For you or the sheep?' Nancy asked without looking at him, her voice tightening.

'Both, I suppose. Raul swore and urged Salvador to keep changing lanes and leave the road as soon as possible. But there was no getting away in the slow-moving traffic, and the sheep kept bleating, and people kept staring.'

'I'm enjoying your discomfort,' Nancy said, almost smiling. 'I hope it lasted all the way to Sydney.'

'It did. Salvador mentioned the law, and Raul's ears turned bright red. He'd been terrified of the police ever since he got on a bus carrying a second-hand door he found at the rubbish tip, and he got in an argument with a passenger who sided with the conductor, and who happened to be an off-duty policeman.

'Eventually, we left the road and stopped in a small car park behind a low building with ads for Coke and Bushel's tea and Marlboro cigarettes on the walls, and the doors and windows were all boarded up with corrugated iron. Raul got out, and in no time at all he'd slit the sheep's throats, and got back in the car still wiping his bloody pocket knife on the rug.

'Then you were back on the road, drinking wine and playing music,' Nancy said, without looking at him. Alfonso noticed her fingers were tightly gripping the steering wheel.

'Yes, but not for long. The bleating had stopped, but in the crowded traffic, someone told us that there was a trail of blood leaking from the Valiant's rusty boot.'

They did not speak for a long while.

It was already dark when they got to Charles Street. Nancy lit the stove and lifted the red pot out of the fridge. She asked Alfonso for greens and laughed when he brought out only potatoes, carrots, onions, and garlic. She peeled the potatoes and carrots standing at the kitchen bench. Alfonso asked what she would like to drink.

'A glass of wine for me and another one for the pot.'

Later he would evoke hazy images of showing Nancy the upstairs part of the house, her calm gaze, their two glasses half-filled with red wine, fogged windowpanes, aromas from the chicken casserole mingling with the sound of the rain outside. One hour, maybe more, indefinitely suspended in his mind, and which he would frequently revisit.

They had just sat down to dinner when the doorbell rang. It was Raul. He had eaten already but agreed to have a drink with them. He sat at the table and commented on the weather. Afterwards he said he was toying with the idea of building a timber and fibro workshop at the back of his house, and he wanted Alfonso's opinion.

Nancy and Alfonso got up and cleared the table, and she put water for coffee on the stove.

While Alfonso and Raul discussed the building of the workshop, she stood at the sink. Alfonso sat facing the window, and he followed the movement of her arms and the items going from one sink bowl to the other and on to the wooden drainer. Glasses first, then knives and forks, then plates and pots, piled dangerously high one on top of another.

She wiped the sink with the yellow dishcloth, spread it over the clean dishes, and took her wine glass to the living room. She switched the TV on, turning the volume up just louder than the men's voices out in the kitchen. When they joined her a while later, still considering the respective qualities of Colourbond and roof tiles, she took her leave.

'It was a good day,' Alfonso said on the way to her car under his umbrella.

'It was.' She smiled and rubbed his upper arm.

'She's made herself queen of the castle,' Raul said when Alfonso returned to the living room.

'What makes you say that?'

'She seems to own the place.'

'She's a friendly person.'

'They are all friendly in the beginning.'

'What are you trying to say?'

'You have a nice place here. You know what happened to Benjamin.'

'You say that because she's Australian?'

'Nationality is not a barrier to their designs.'

'We're just friends.'

'Have it your own way, Alfonso. But don't say you haven't been warned.'

Raul left soon after. Alfonso boiled water, made another coffee, and sat at the kitchen table. He sat there for a long time, playing with the teaspoon in his hands while appeasing a kind of resentment, almost hostility, towards his friend for robbing him of Nancy's company. Raul had no business at the table or in the house. He wished he had told him to stay out of it the moment he started mentioning Nancy, perhaps even when he knocked at the door. So what if he was rude? Good manners worked both ways.

As he deposited the empty cup in the sink, he saw a small brown cockroach strolling among the dishes Nancy had washed earlier. Crazy with sudden fury, he gave chase, flinging aside dishes until he pursued it into the cutlery basket. He tipped the contents of the basket in the sink, opened the hot water tap, and observed the roach's futile struggle to stay alive.

The following weekend Nancy was busy being a bridesmaid. She dropped by on the next Tuesday on her way from work. She said she was studying for her bookkeeping exams and wouldn't stay long. But she would have a coffee, and produced a packet of assorted biscuits from her carry bag to go with it.

They sat at the kitchen table. She asked about his work. There had been reports in the papers and on TV regarding a service lift crashing to the ground at a Darling Point construction site, killing two people and injuring several others. There were safety concerns in the building industry. She was anxious for him.

There was a short silence. Then she got up, walked around the table and sat on his knees. He put his arms around her waist. She reminded him of her trip to England, that she would be away for six weeks, and said that she would miss him. Then she took his face in her hands and kissed him tenderly on the forehead, and on the eyes, and the mouth, and the ears.

Ten minutes later, she was gone. But the scent of her hair and her body stayed, and Alfonso, unable to sit or stand still, wandered from the living room to the kitchen and back again, breathing deeply.

The next day Alfonso woke with a mild headache. It got worse on the way to the building site on the Lower North Shore. During the morning break, the smell of his salami sandwiches made him nauseous, so he put them away. At lunch, he took only the coffee thermos out of his bag, and his workmates made fun of him.

'He's pale as death,' said Domenico.

'Shagging is better left for the weekend,' added Barry.

'Leave him alone,' pleaded Nick. 'Can't you see he is coming down with something?'

In the course of the afternoon, his hammer grew heavier. On his way to Charles Street, he felt as if every one of his aching joints were welded to the rattling train.

He walked at a slow pace from the station to the house, took a shower, and lay on the couch, staring at the ceiling, wondering what was sucking the strength from his body but leaving his mind so calm.

After an hour or so, he boiled some potatoes and carrots, which he ate with fried eggs, then he did the dishes and went to bed. Sleep overtook him right away, and he dreamed he was fetching onions for his mother from the semi-dark room above the stables that was rumoured to be inhabited by poisonous spiders.

He woke in the morning with a terribly sore throat. His image in the bathroom mirror reminded him of an old village neighbour dead for two days in the winter rain. He made it to the phone in the kitchen and dialled work.

'I'm not well,' he said to Andrew, the supervisor.

'What is wrong?'

'I don't know.'

'Well, I don't bloody know either. You're the third bugger to report sick this morning.'

'What do you want me to do?'

'Get off the damn phone.'

Alfonso drank a glass of water and went back to bed. The garbage truck arrived outside the house. He wished the collectors made less noise and showed the bins some mercy. Then he thought of his friends in the change room at work in various states of undress, feet on newspapers. At the site office, Andrew would be swearing at everyone and everything until the morning tasks got into a rhythm.

He slept for a few hours. When he woke, in addition to his sore throat and stiff limbs, his left ear was throbbing. Then he remembered Celestina, a young woman in his village, who had one day complained of a pain in her arm. The pain had multiplied into many pains. Medical help was eight kilometres away. It was winter, and the village's unpaved road made it inaccessible by car. Inhaling vapours from boiled eucalyptus, administering enemas, and poultices... All were tried. Her screams, sharp as broken glass, went on for two and half days before the money and a horse for the doctor were found. He came and suppressed the screaming. And her life, people said.

The long, noisy deliberations of a number of crows meeting on the verandah's roof outside his bedroom irritated him. Then irritation was replaced by uneasiness and he decided to seek help. He took a short shower and walked slowly to Oxford Street, where he caught a bus to Bondi Junction. The bus was half empty. He sat near the back, listened to the beating in his right ear, and stared blankly at the comb restraining the golden hair of a woman sitting two rows ahead of him.

Dr Suarez's surgery was on the ground floor of a two-storey house.

'Do you have an appointment?' asked the receptionist.

'No.'

'Have you been here before?'

'No.'

'Name and address?'

She typed the details onto a white card. There was no expression on her well-formed face, and he thought that the squeak of her swivel chair and the hammer of her typewriter were synchronised.

'Please take a seat.'

He sat on a hard, straight-backed chair. He noted the healthy potted plant on the table by the door. The large, white-painted walls of the room were naked, the plaster ceilings elaborate. To his left, a tall window looked out on a paved courtyard. Soft music wafted from speakers he could not locate. A low table with magazines separated him from the other patients, a man and two women. The man wore heavy-framed glasses and breathed in and out of his mouth. The women had their hands on their laps and looked like sisters. None of the three were young. Their expressions reminded Alfonso of tired horses. He closed his eyes and must have slept, for there were new people in the room when he opened them again, and his name was being called.

The grey-haired doctor asked Alfonso to open his mouth and say 'ah', peered into his ears, and put his stethoscope to his chest and back. Then he sat at his desk and started writing.

'I am giving you antibiotics and a week off work,' he said.

'A week?'

'Yes.'

'But I ...'

'You have a nasty cold. But my main concern is with your even nastier ear infection.' He took off his glasses and stood up. 'Drink lots of fruit juice and have plenty rest,' he said, and handed Alfonso the prescription.

On the return trip, Alfonso got off the bus at Taylor Square and went into a pharmacy. While the chemist put together his medication, he walked across the road to a grocer and bought orange juice and some apples and bananas. Back in Charles Street, he called work and left a message for his supervisor.

In his bedroom, he undressed and lay down. Soon he began to shiver, then to sweat. He dreamed he was lost in a dense forest of giant pines with red fig leaves and loud croaking frogs with black skin, some with only one eye. In another dream, he floated up to a corner of the room under the ceiling, crouched down on his haunches, and gazed at his body lying on the bed below. The face had a peaceful look; dark patches framed the eyes. It needed a shave. The penis, yellowed like the rest of the body, lay at an angle and appeared smaller than he remembered. He was wearing brown shoes without socks. Perhaps, he thought, they had washed him and were to dress him when the call had come for lunch and Benito, a neighbour with a sense of humour to fit all occasions, did not want him to have cold feet. The shoes were new, and he remembered Sacundino saying that sometimes shoes were purchased for the occasion and removed, along with ornamental handles, just before the coffin was lowered into the ground. He also said that the dead came back to earth to see who was wearing the shoes.

Alfonso woke to the weekend paperboy's whistle. Faces, voices, lingered in his memory: Dr Suarez sitting at the desk writing a certificate for work, a very pregnant woman in the chemist's shop … but he could not recall getting back to the house, nor did he remember anything of Friday or Saturday.

For a while he just lay in bed, quietly confused. He was further baffled when he rose to his feet and saw spilt orange juice on the carpet by the bed and a trail of vomit leading to the bathroom. He descended slowly to the kitchen and looked at the calendar hanging on the wall between the phone and the fridge. He took the red ballpoint pen from the top of the fridge and crossed Thursday off. Then he walked to the living room, clicked on the TV, and searched through the channels for the hour of prayer and choir singing on ABC to confirm that it was Sunday.

'Two days and three nights in bed and I am still alive?' he asked, eying the calendar and then the pills, the eardrops, and the syrup on the kitchen table, untouched.

He washed his face in cold water at the kitchen sink. It was a bright day. His eyes hurt as he looked out the window, and his legs trembled at the knees, but he felt no pain.

He woke on the couch in the middle of the afternoon with the local paper on his chest, unwrapped, and a cold coffee on the table. His head was crowded with images of the coloured pills he had swallowed earlier, of the green fluid in the ear dropper suspended above his ear, of Nancy walking in a park under very old trees, of his old friend Guapo napping on a yellow and white beach towel. These remembered images, silent and frozen, seemed like photos already taken but not developed. 'Did the mind ever sleep?' he asked himself. The answer came almost immediately in the form of a picture of the state of his bedroom.

He smiled, rose from the couch, went to the laundry for a bucket, sponge and detergent, and made his way upstairs. Squatting at first, then on his hands and knees, he cleaned up the mess. He washed and scrubbed the area three times. He wondered if it would leave a stain. After replacing the crumpled bed sheets and the bloodied pillowcase, he undressed for the shower. The soap and hot water felt good on his body, save for the sharp pain coming from his skull when he tried to wash his hair.

Stirrings of hunger came as he dried himself. But by the time he grilled two pieces of bread with cheese and tomatoes, switched on the TV for the nightly news, and sat down to eat, he was no longer hungry. And the food tasted of blood. Yet, aware of his weakened condition, he continued chewing slowly and mechanically. Half an hour later, he was violently sick at the kitchen sink.

He made it back to bed. He heard his name being called. He recognised the owl that once lived in the attic of his village schoolhouse, followed the bird's gaze, and saw that the occasional morning patch of grey mist over the river had thickened, darkened, and spread to the cornfields, meadows, and pine groves.

He slept well and woke near noon on Monday. After taking a shower, he looked in the fridge and in the tall cupboard for something that would not upset his stomach, and settled for a can of chicken and vegetable soup.

There was no taste in the soup, but the good smell of toasted bread was back, he thought as he lay on the couch afterwards. His body heavy, yet pleasantly lethargic, his mind quiet, he looked forward to the sleep that he knew would come the moment he closed his eyes.

Shrill sounds from the nearby school interrupted an old recurring dream in which one weekend in early summer, the young boys of the village would raid as many birds' nests as they could find, and the girls, supervised by young women still unmarried, would cook several egg and potato omelettes in the kitchen of the old school house.

He could still see the varied colour patterns and shapes of the eggs piled high on the large wooden bowl. One year he had gathered the most eggs. He was proud, but his mother said it was cruel. She also pointed to his torn trousers, the result of climbing the trees.

Thirsty, Alfonso got up to fetch a glass of water and thought about the noises that would visit the house every morning and afternoon while he was at work. There were the resident noises he was familiar with, various boards on the stairs that always complained bitterly when stepped on, and a couple of them in his bedroom that moaned like empty hearts. At night, with the windows open, the buzz of the city filled the rooms with a murmur much like that the sound of the waters in the village stream. On Sunday mornings, the church bells were brought to life. In the afternoon, there was the soft click of the brass mail slot, followed by the pamphlet man slamming the front gate behind him.

Not long after he returned to the couch with the water, the afternoon sun made its way through the back window, lighting up one section of the room while the other grew dark. Shadows, like noises, were houseguests, free to come and go as they pleased. He most liked the moon showing from behind the houses across the road and advancing into his bedroom. There followed a straggle of friendly moonlit shapes, unlike the shadows of the headstones of the village cemetery that continually cowered and quivered under tree branches that, on windy nights, whispered like damned souls and made his hair stand on end every time he walked by.

When the radio announcer on 2CH had read the headlines for the six o'clock news, he went to the kitchen and boiled potatoes, carrots, and two eggs, which he mixed with tuna, oil, and vinegar. He ate in the kitchen, returning to the living room to watch television. Later, going up the stairs, he felt as though his legs weighed fifty kilos each, but the feeling that he was about to fall had gone, and while brushing his teeth, he noticed that his gums didn't bleed as much.

He got into bed and took up his book, but instead of reading, he put out the bedside lamp and gazed at the pictures of Nancy hanging about in his memory. Almost immediately, an indefinable feeling distracted him. He had felt it earlier, in the kitchen while administering the eardrops, but then it had been just a faint agitation like a gentle breeze on a sleeping cornfield. Now it was insistent, like an itch. He tried to spool his memory back to its specific source.

Late one afternoon, two days before her accounting exams and subsequent departure for England, Nancy had come to say goodbye. They had sat at the kitchen table, talking, drinking coffee, and eating biscuits. Afterwards, she had come to his side of the table and sat on his lap. They had embraced. They had kissed for the first time. He distinctly remembered her breasts, hard and alive, against his chest, and her warm breath and moist lips in his ear.

He had compared those intimate, precious minutes to the winter's reserve of honey in a beehive, from which they could feed during their separation. Now, he thought it was strange how quickly they had fallen for one another. Then he felt unease, haunted by a vague fear of a connection between Nancy's kisses and his ear infection. He lay very still in the silent and darkened room.

The next memory he recalled was of a weekend with Raul putting down a new floor in a house in Glebe. The owner, Gerardo, forty, thin and foul-breathed, was helping them.

'Is the new floor for the wedding?' Raul had asked Gerardo at lunchtime.

'I don't think so,' Gerardo laughed. 'Women are dangerous.'

'Gentle lambs with the patience of spiders,' Raul said and laughed, too.

'Float like butterflies, sting like a bees, we say where I come from,' Gerardo said. They both laughed again.

All afternoon they worked and enumerated various female traps and treacheries. Both agreed that women arranged everything for their own purposes. Both concluded that women's hearts contained the single ambition of a house and kids, and husbands were like disposable shaving blades.

Alfonso did not agree. The ambitions of women were like their bodies and their smells, he thought, some good, some less so. But he decided to say nothing. As Sacundino would say, 'Keeping the mouth shut is good for the wise and even better for the stupid.' Besides, Raul had sponsored him to Australia, met him at the dock, and provided him with tools and accommodation for twelve weeks, in which time he had not been allowed to contribute to living expenses or stop Remedios, Raul's wife, from washing and ironing his clothes. It was a kindness he would always remember.

Raul's opinions were not rational. Alfonso had not forgotten the night Raul had ruined dinner with Nancy, or his comments after she had left. What could he possibly know, seeing her just once at the barbecue? He wished not to have bad feelings for his friend, but he still felt annoyed with himself, bitter almost, for not having told him to shut up. And he suspected that something from that night, something boding no good, was still haunting him.

Alfonso wished sleep would come to turn off the scenarios playing in his head. The black-faced alarm clock read quarter past twelve. Its loud ticking annoyed him, and he decided to buy a clock radio the next time he was at Paddy's Market so he could go to sleep in silence and be woken by music. Switching on the bedside lamp, he drank some orange juice straight from the plastic container on the floor. A bright ring of white light at the base of the lamp mirrored a larger ring on the ceiling. Everything else in the room took on the orange of the lampshade. The bare walls needed something, he thought. His mother would have hung a crucifix over the bed, a coloured picture of the Madonna and Child, and one of the Last Supper somewhere else in the house. That would be the minimum requirement to ward off evil spirits entering the house.

Did Nancy pray? He would ask her when she came back. Maybe not. In Australia, many subjects were labelled personal. He would just ask her to choose something pleasant and inexpensive to hang here and there. Also, curtains, and knives, and glasses. He had been embarrassed on the day of the barbecue for not having enough to go around.

He began to think of his mother. Although she had been distressed, she understood he needed to go away, and he felt remorse for not having written regularly while she was alive. He had done so in the beginning, then stopped. And it had been near impossible to start again. But he had not forgotten her recurring belly pains, her struggle to make ends meet, her eyes red-rimmed in the morning from praying or from crying, or both. Every Christmas, he had sent her a cheque for $500.

'Keep the money,' she would reply. 'Write. Tell us how you are doing. Pray for your father.' Her one-page letters would have taken her two long nights to write.

He turned to face the wall. The little dots left by the paint roller reminded him of the stone wall, rough and full of crevices, that faced the bed with the noisy straw mattress he had shared with his brother. In that wall, he had seen peaceful valleys, wild horses, ponds teeming with fish of all colours and shapes, shadowy forests from which no one came back, scary faces and grim shapes.

He put out the bedside light and lay on his back to wait for sleep. Instead he heard murmurings, voices and images from other nights long in the past. One scene followed another. He was still a young boy, at night, in the middle of the long winter. They had already dined, done the dishes, and recited the Rosary. He was then allowed to visit a school friend whose parents had much land, a big kitchen, and plenty of wood for the fire. Six, seven, eight neighbours gathered there every evening. At one end of the room, the men played cards at a long wooden table. At the other end, the women sat on wooden benches by the open fire telling stories, listening, knitting, or dozing. Outside the dogs barked, the wind gnawed at the trees and the house, and the wolves howled. Fire shadows danced on the kitchen walls as if in tune with the telling and retelling of stories: tormented animas roaming the earth, satanic envoys hunting for souls, men and women buried alive, children born with scales and tails and sold to circuses of freaks and cripples, never to be heard from again. Stories about aphrodisiac ointments and syrups for maddening passion were Alfonso's favourites. The pictures of men with bulging trousers, possessed by desire, stayed with him long after he left childhood.

For those afflicted by such passion, medicos prescribed enemas and bloodletting. The priest recommended cold baths, sleeping on beds of thorns and thistles, and wearing scapulars made from the bones of saints. The wealthy had access to the bishop and were treated to the recitation of special passages from missals, written with the blood of virgins. But once the spell was cast, the bewitched stayed bewitched. More often than not, the cures increased their cravings rather than decreasing them. The only cure for the unbearable pang of desire was carnal possession, and that only after the marriage formalities were completed.

Bernarda was Alfonso's favourite storyteller. She was toothless, and her voice came out strange, and unnatural. Her tales had a ring of authenticity because she happened to have known someone who knew someone who had been present. Awesome women figured prominently in her narratives. But they were not the usual spell casters or palm readers, predicting the future for a fee on market day. Her women were recluses with faces withered like prunes, elongated teeth, beak-like noses, and white hair. They were the friends of women who had been wronged and forgotten. Their covert powers and knowledge had been transferred from one generation to another. They made use of both icons and black candles. In winter, and always under the kind of full moon that sent dogs crazy, they trapped snakes, toads, lizards, and spiders. In spring they collected wild herbs, mushrooms, and furze flowers. From their labour came concoctions that led to the loss of teeth and hair, or brought on stammers, hiccups, and other afflictions. They delivered their wares through wine or food in a tavern, a charm slipped into a coat pocket, or the saliva of a kiss.

He woke at five on Wednesday, just before the clamour of the alarm clock. The timekeeper within his head was working again, he thought, as he drifted back to sleep and into the sensory memories of his childhood.

He got up at up midday, hungry. There were no tomatoes or bacon in the fridge. The egg carton was empty and the milk was sour, but there were some potatoes, a full tin of olive oil in the cupboard, and meat in the freezer.

After a snack of bread and sardines, he washed the plates and cups left in the sink from previous days. He went to the backyard, apologised to the parsley plant for his absence, raked its soil, and watered it gently. He lavished the same care on the grapevine and the lemon and mandarin trees. The fig tree had suffered the most.

Sweeping the terracotta tiles, he felt an ache just beneath his heart and sat down. It was anxiety, not physical pain, gripping his chest. Concerned by the direction of his thoughts, he went back in, did the washing, and vacuumed the house, guiding the nozzle into every possible nook and crevice. Finally he opened the windows to let fresh air in and all the nonsense in his head out.

For dinner, he took two small pork chops from the freezer. He dropped them in hot water in the sink and peeled the potatoes. The chops had turned an ugly grey as he dried them on a tea towel, but they recovered in the grill.

He cleared the table and sat down to watch TV, but he could not concentrate. He stood up and restlessly wandered the upstairs rooms of the house and the verandah. He took the garbage out. The stars twinkled in the sky, his garments hung motionless below. He listened sympathetically to the cats yowling in the lane. There was again taste in his mouth, a good sign that his body was mending, but his thoughts were like tangled fishing line.

There were two universes inside his head, and it seemed that the demarcation between the two had dissolved, allowing the old one to infect the new. Yet, he felt there was no room in Australia for scapulars around the neck, for amulets under the bed, for birds carrying urgent warnings from the dead. The illness had stripped away his common sense, permitting superstitions to roam a feverish mind in a body still recovering from something he could not name or understand.

He woke on Thursday with the sun already in the room. He remembered that there was no milk or bread in the house and that he was due back at work the next day. It was pleasant to wash his hair but painful to shave his week-old beard. He lathered a second time, changed the blade, but still it hurt. He smiled wryly at his trembling hand for making such hard work of saving a few days' growth.

Downstairs, after collecting the local newspaper and junk mail from the mat in the hallway, he walked to the corner store at the end of the street. The air was clear and smelled of something new.

The shopkeeper, a short, round man, was telling a customer how someone had pinched a bundle of *Daily Telegraph*s from his doorstep that morning. He repeated the incident to Alfonso as he put milk, eggs, and bread in a bag, and held on to the change until he'd finished the telling.

Back in the house, Alfonso called the site office.

'Take Friday off,' said Andrew, his supervisor.

Alfonso thanked him, replaced the receiver, and on the wall calendar drew a line that joined together all the days he'd been ill.

Many things can happen in a week, he thought as he fried eggs and bacon for lunch. He carried his plate to the coffee table. Tarzan and Jane were on the TV. The location in the movie looked similar to a remote part of the village where he had trapped rabbits. It was a sheltered bend in the river where the water was still and deep as a lake, yet so clear that one could see every multicoloured pebble. Girls and young women bathed there in summer. From a safe distance, he and other boys would hide in the bushes and watch them frolicking in the water or lying on the grass.

The outline of their bodies, their fascinating whiteness, became summer memories to be visited over and over.

Summer snapshots scrolled though his memory. Summer was wonderful, he thought. It dried the thick stone walls of the houses, warmed the bones of the elderly, stirred up red passions in the young with evening dances. The earth showed off its apples, corn, rye, hay, and potatoes. The heavens put on magnificent shows of lightning and thunder, women and children gathered in candlelit rooms to pray to St Barbara for protection, and supposedly brave men hid under mattresses like shivering rabbits.

On Monday, Alfonso got to work early. He changed into fresh work clothes, putting the dirty ones in a plastic bag to take home. While he was thoroughly inspecting his boots for spiders, the supervisor appeared in the doorway, asked him how he was, and gave him job instructions.

That day he was working on the fifth floor, completing the lift well and fire stairs to the sixth. Low clouds obscured the sun, and the wind was sharp, but he worked well and the hours passed quickly.

During the lunch break, Domenico commented that he thought Alfonso had lost weight. Someone else said he looked pale. Alfonso perceived concern in their voices and appreciated it. On the train, he reflected on how much he had enjoyed the day's work and the company of his friends.

It was good to be back home, too. The shower washed away his tiredness. The plants seemed to reach out to him as he watered them. The wine tasted good. Dinner was easy with so much to choose from after his shopping trip to Paddy's on Saturday morning. He went to bed early, taking with him an issue of the *Reader's Digest*, but he did not read it. In the dark he thought of his health, which until now had not bothered him, and Nancy, and a new life ahead.

The letter from Nancy arrived on Wednesday. Alfonso opened it in the kitchen and read it. He read it again while eating chicken and potatoes left over from the previous night, and later in bed, this time aloud.

She wrote of castles made of clouds below the plane's window, of her cousin's wedding, of how she was now staying with her widowed aunt in Bristol, of how the house, full of old furniture and bric-a-brac, stood opposite a park with big trees. They drank gin and tonic or sherry before dinner. She liked England, but was not sure she could live there. She said 'I miss you' at the end of the letter. Her handwriting was small and pretty.

He had been in England once, for several hours, on his way to Australia. In a café at the train station in London, Ovidio, his sad acquaintance, had described life in exile, and had reminded Alfonso not to stay away too long or he would belong nowhere. Wishing not to dwell on the man's advice, he thought he should buy a ticket to fly to Melbourne or Canberra or some other city, just to experience what it was like to be in the air. Airplanes were part of his early memories. One flew over the village at ten o'clock in the morning and at five in the afternoon. It was a reliable timekeeper. Then he smiled, remembering how the dogs barked at its shadow moving on the ground.

The second letter arrived ten days later. This time she wrote less of her and more of him. 'Do you eat properly? Is your workplace safe?' He put the letter back in the envelope and placed it on the mantelpiece with the other.

That night he heard his mother's voice. Her tone was softer than he remembered and seemed to come from far away. She liked Nancy. They didn't have the bond of a common culture, but they were both young and could bridge the distance. She described a good marriage; after a while, after the novelty wore off, it became a bit like a game of give and take. And a bad marriage was an unequal contest. Of course, Nancy was a city-bred girl, and her kind could be expensive with their penchant for shampoos and permanents and holidays away, but she also worked, she paid her way. Mother didn't like Raul. 'He is a know-it-all peasant of the worst kind,' she added.

In the third letter, Nancy's feelings were no longer guarded. 'I want to be with you always,' the words underlined. He liked that very much and read it once more in the morning before leaving for work.

A couple of days later, he had eaten dinner and was reading on the couch when the doorbell rang. It was Pavel. He happened to be in the area quoting for a plumbing job. He had news about Pascual, a mutual friend from the days when they did casual weekend work for an Italian builder. 'Eleven years in Australia,' the plumber said. 'Nice house in Paddington, good looking wife, two children, and a dog. He is now to too proud to call on his friends so he sleeps in the car.'

'What happened?' Alfonso asked.

'It looks like they started quarrelling. You guess the rest,' said Pavel.

Alfonso knew what 'the rest' meant. Apparently, a new family law had made divorce easier. A man at work said that breaking up was now fashionable. Another man complained that the new law was a joke: it gave women the upper hand.

After a second glass of wine, Pavel left. Alfonso cut tomatoes for the sandwiches for work and thought of what the plumber had said. It was not for him to decide who was right or wrong, but he knew that Pascual lived for his family. It saddened him to imagine his friend in the back of the station wagon, curled up under newspapers on a chilly night like an old derelict in Woolloomooloo. That was terrible, he reasoned. He would quietly look for him. There was a spare room upstairs where he could mend his pride, hide his shame, or both.

While brushing his teeth, he remembered Raul saying, 'Divorces and funerals are wives' ultimate weddings.' Later, lying in bed, he shut his eyes and replayed the pictures of Nancy stored in his memory. She was at the barbecue, laughing at a joke from Pedro; she was collecting wild flowers in the Blue Mountains. As the images unfolded one after the other, he became aware as never before that Nancy was the unconscious dream, the cherished ideal that had sustained him in the village, through his homesickness of the first years in Australia, learning English, rebuilding the house. She was the future he had always wanted.

After a time, he slept. Yet his mind kept on working, generating bizarre images of his house being broken into and the Western red cedar internal doors, kitchen cupboards, and fireplace surroundings removed while he was at work. Raul stood across the road, a faint smile on his face. In the morning, he reassured himself it was his imagination playing games when it should be resting. But by mid-afternoon, he thought that the images were too vivid to be ignored, that they could well be a premonition of his future.

And for a week or so he was haunted by contradictory emotions, nourished by Nancy's smile and frightened by Raul's words at the gate that 'a woman is the path to both Heaven and Hell.'

A couple of days later, a bird shat on him while he was walking to North Sydney train station. He cleaned his face and hair in the station's bathroom and caught the next train. He stood just to the right of the door, one hand on the leather strap hanging from the ceiling of the train, as his thoughts shuffled with the bad omen, his legs weakened by sudden panic.

Back in Charles Street, he unpacked his bag at the kitchen bench, poured himself a glass of wine, and sat on the stone bench at the back. Low clouds changed from red to grey on the horizon. The children playing in the lane were called indoors for dinner. Then, quite suddenly, he knew that his relationship with Nancy had to end. The feeling of relief was immediate. He got up, went to the kitchen, and poured another glass of wine. He made the sandwiches for work and two extra that he ate before going to bed.

He slept well, undisturbed by dreams. Work was on the seventh floor. Under a bright sky, ferries and sailing boats crisscrossed the harbour. He worked efficiently and had enough spare time and patience to suggest the correct ways of doing things to the second-year apprentice Andrew had sent to work with him, rather than merely fixing up his mistakes.

Halfway through the afternoon, a strong wind appeared from over the water, then a disturbing thought: Nancy would soon be back from England and she would have to be told. How was he going to do it? Was he going to tell her face-to-face? Was he going to write her a letter? Was he going to use the phone? And, most importantly, what was he going to say?

He was anxious not to offend or hurt her in any way. He had never lied in his life. 'Lies stain the soul,' his mother used to say. But what was the truth? Was he to say he had to act on premonitions of future happenings that could be prevented? And if she asked, 'What happened?' would he mention his fear of shame, anger, the indignity of a failed marriage, divorce settlements, love potions, warnings wrapped in bird droppings, and other nonsense infecting his thinking?

Another week passed. He remained troubled and vaguely aware that he was mixing truth and dream, reality and the imaginary, and that he was incapable of differentiating one from the other.

On Saturday afternoon, he was in the kitchen putting away the weekly shopping when the telephone rang. It rang a second time while he was ironing a shirt and a third after he went to bed. It didn't occur to him that it might be someone other than Nancy. He felt an irresistible longing to hear her voice, but he could not control the violent panic that stopped him from lifting the receiver.

There was a knock on the door early on Sunday evening. Alfonso was having dinner and ignored it. A second knock minutes later had an added urgency, and he got up to answer it. Halfway down the hallway he turned around, went up to his bedroom, and parted the curtains a fraction to spy on the street below.

The verandah blocked his view of the front door, but he stood as if nailed to the floor until he heard the gate slam shut and a car start up and drive away. He put away his half-finished meal. Pretending he was not home had made him sick. Dawn found him sitting in the yard, elbows on his knees, head resting on his hands.

He went to the kitchen and put the kettle on for coffee. He did not shower, shave, or eat breakfast before setting off for the train station. Stricken by raw shame and anger, blighted by sleeplessness, he struggled through the morning. During the midday break, he avoided his friends with the excuse that he had to go to a nearby hardware store. The afternoon passed slowly. He could think of nothing except what a coward he was.

On his way home each afternoon, he had always gazed at the Opera House through the train window. Today the strange excitement of its beauty changed to ache. He was relieved when the train entered the tunnel under the city. Now he understood why dogs sought a dark place to heal or to die.

That evening he paced the yard, his thoughts knotted up on what he had done to a good woman, to his life, to his decency. And in the kitchen, potatoes and carrots boiled over the stove, and veal chops turned to leather under the grill.

Part Three

Chapter 1

On Monday morning, Alfonso looked out the kitchen window. Thick mist hung in the air, and it was still dark. He finished his coffee and left for work.

He closed the front door and crossed the patio. As he opened the gate, he spotted Nancy standing half-hidden from the street lighting beneath the branches of the tree in front of the house. They stood for a moment; neither of them spoke. Then she turned around, walked to her car, and drove away. Alfonso remained a while longer, staring at the ground in front of his shoes, then went inside and paced back and forth in his living room, his hands shaking, his mind numb. Ten minutes later, he poured water over his head at the kitchen sink and headed off to work.

A week earlier, he had searched for the right words to convey his decision to her, believing in the saying, 'A punch is forgotten, but a word never.' It had not occurred to him then that he would utilise silence, the language of the wise and the cowardly.

During the whole day, his concentration wavered and he made mistakes, one serious. After work, he avoided the farewell drinks for a retiring colleague at a nearby pub. His workmates attributed both incidents to his recent illness.

On his way to the station, he looked for the bird that had shat on him not so long ago. He no longer believed it was carrying a message from the future. The bird was simply attending to its business and he, Alfonso, could make whatever he wanted of it.

He got off the train at Central Station as usual. Instead of taking his customary route, he walked down one side street and then another, in order to enter the house through the back gate and so avoid the image of Nancy standing under the tree, arms by her sides, sad, mute, and motionless. He used the back gate for many days. He did not look out the verandah. At work, high on level ten, he often paused, shaded his eyes with a hand, and looked out the direction of the distant Blue Mountains. He thought how proud and happy he had been, walking by her side in the natural splendour of the caves, sitting with her at the café.

Her presence was stronger at night. In bed he had just to close his eyelids for her to appear sitting at the table, or standing at the sink peeling potatoes, or walking on the beach. She was everywhere, a woodpecker tapping at his consciousness.

It rained on Sunday night. The kitchen windowpanes, fogged by the lentil soup cooking on the stove, reminded him of that fine evening on their return from the trip to the Blue Mountains, and how Raul's visit had spoiled everything. In bed that night, in his sleep, tears ran down his cheeks.

A fortnight passed. Alfonso's shock from the encounter with Nancy subsided, but he remained deeply shamed and troubled by his behaviour.

He sought an escape in work. As Sacundino used to say, 'There is nothing that work or fishing will not cure.' So each day, from seven o'clock to three-thirty in the afternoon, he went to his main job, then to a second job with an Italian builder until seven. Returning home he took a shower, boiled potatoes and carrots and grilled chops for dinner, did the dishes, and went to bed. Strange dreams fractured his sleep and he awoke in the morning tired and confused.

He saw few friends and did not encourage visitors. And so another fortnight passed. Although the physical Nancy was no longer part of his life, the absent one kept on watching.

One Sunday, he attended his supervisor's birthday barbecue in Annandale. Andrew, the same age as Alfonso, had married Lucy four years before. They had a one-year-old boy, a two-year-old girl, and Lucy was pregnant. Soon after his arrival, Lucy introduced him to Emily. She was a brunette, tall and pretty. Did he work with Andrew? How long had he been in Australia, she asked? She was a nurse. She and Lucy were school friends. Later, at the kitchen counter over coffee and cakes, they had another chat. Before leaving, she said she hoped to see him again.

Driving home in the late afternoon, he thought of his friend and his wife and their lovely children, and wondered if they knew how lucky they were. Then he thought of Emily. He sensed he had made a good impression. He usually did, he believed without vanity. Friends saw him as a pleasant and decent man, one who preferred to listen than to talk, one who was at peace with the world. Then he wondered what would they have thought if they knew of his private life. Or his unrelenting awareness that he had ruined in an instant the gift of love that mysterious fate had taken years to deliver?

Back in Charles Street, he hung his clothes in the cupboard and put on a pair of shorts and a t-shirt. In the kitchen, he set out the bread, ham, cheese, and tomatoes to make the sandwiches for work the next day. He stopped now and then to think about Nancy, then returned to the sandwiches. He imagined himself going in search of her and making reparations. He wished there was someone he could talk to about it. But who? Some of his workmates were domestic despots. The cynics would laugh and remind him 'how much a man gained when he lost a good woman.' The tailor would have understood, but he was gone. Pavel had amorous troubles of his own. The brothers would hear him and laugh and think he had a screw loose. They accepted the merits of marriage, the risks, and the boredom of copulating on set days of the week in the conventional position. Anything else made no sense to them.

Most of his friends had no time for women as anything other than a maid. He clearly recalled how, in some households in his village, women were treated no better than the livestock. Then he thought of his childhood, with just his brother and mother, her female friends and her two older sisters, who visited twice a year. Friends and aunts were generous and kind, despite disagreement about one thing or another. Mother used to say that the world would be a nicer place if women had been listened to. She would also caution his brother, every time he went to labour for the bricklayers in a nearby town or city, not to fall for the girls there. When Alfonso had asked her why, she said a wife from those places would not make the adjustment to life in the village.

Adjustment was an interesting word, he said to himself as he put the sandwich in the lunchbox. But the concept made him uneasy without his understanding it fully, and he tried to push it out of his mind by watching a movie on television.

In the morning, the word was still in his mind. His old friend the tailor believed he could never fit into the Australian way of life because he was trapped in another world, another time, another place. The chisel-maker often said that it was in his heart where the new world met with the old. The two worlds did not get on and were always bickering with each other. The same with Raul and others long gone. And it came as a kind of surprise that it might relate to him also.

He was at ease with the customs. He was even comfortable wearing thongs. He remained ever grateful for the decent work and material goods the country had provided him. But these external manifestations, these noble sentiments alone did not prove him to be Australian, or define what it meant to be Australian, as his muddled reasoning behind Nancy's dismissal clearly demonstrated.

Then he remembered Antonio García, an acquaintance from the early days, who took Australian citizenship, wore long socks and ironed shorts, changed his name to Fred Smith, and used the word 'mate' with strongly Spanish-accented English. But it was all artificial and just made him a figure of fun, Alfonso thought.

No, he reasoned on his way to work, adjustment was an internal matter, an inward thing he couldn't quite grasp.

Two further weeks went by. Alfonso's mood and thoughts were less sour. His relationships with women were a parade of bruises, errors, yet he felt tenderness for them, and their bodies continued to fascinate him. In a rare moment of confidence, he told himself that each day was a fresh start, that Lady Luck was capricious and, if given a chance, she might call again.

Reassured by this spark of encouragement, he resumed going out on Saturday nights. But something had now changed. The nightclub music was louder and faster. His new friends, with one or two exceptions, were a different kind of migrant: younger, educated, pragmatic. They were in Australia to look around, free to leave, free to stay. But the rituals remained. They would gather at the Spanish Club bar, have dinner, and then depart for the Concordia or the Apia clubs. Towards midnight, those still unpaired would depart for other places, hoping for easy pickings.

Alfonso would stay a little longer, buy a drink, and watch the dancers, pretending not to.

Although he was not much older than they were, he often found himself at a loss in their company. Sometimes he felt that he didn't fit in, wondering if he had already aged beyond his years. At parties where people danced and laughed and drank, he wished he was somewhere else. He usually left early.

As a youth in the village, he had imagined that dancing was an excuse for groin-to-groin contact. Now he thought that it confirmed reciprocal attraction, and that the eroticism of dance was one of the spiritual secrets of romance. He liked the slow shuffling of feet, bodies touching, which allowed illusion to spread through the senses. Sometimes he danced several numbers with one partner. Although he always finished the night on his own, those brief encounters on the dance floor generated optimism. But the excitement of these beginnings was quickly replaced by fear, as he thought of the inherent danger in every woman, of what a woman in time might become.

The sense of futility was unavoidable. 'I court a woman one week and then run away from her the next,' he said to himself one evening as he undressed and put his pants and jacket in the wardrobe. 'I'm wasting everybody's time.' He brushed his teeth and got into bed. Behind his closed eyelids, Nancy appeared. She was like a shadow tugging at him, silently identifying the flaws in each of the women he met: this one has thick calves, that one has narrow shoulders, the other one smokes too much.

Unable to sleep or to distinguish what was real inside his head, he got up and went to the kitchen, filled a glass of water and sat at the kitchen table. The house was silent, dense black outside. His feelings were the same as they had been in the village every time he knelt before Father Manuel to confess his sins.

Not that Father Manuel was hard towards his penitents. 'Simply the truth, my boy,' he would say.

The father's words also applied now, Alfonso thought, if he were prepared to look into the dark recesses of his mind.

From the small pile of papers at one end of the table, he took the gas bill envelope and wrote on the back, *Why did I let Nancy go?*

He dismissed the notion that her saliva had bewitched him as superstitious nonsense, an excuse not to face up to his mental wreckage. He no longer saw shame in divorce if a man and woman could not live in harmony, neither did he begrudge the splitting of assets. Most of the men in his circle felt contempt for women, but he did not. Why? Why was he different? Was he ashamed that his manliness was compromised? Was he being loyal to his mates and their ethos? To his mother? Was he afraid of ceasing to be himself if he took on so-called Australian attitudes, afraid of losing his past, his Spanishness, his childhood experiences and memories, if he decided to share his life with a woman who knew nothing of that and might not understand? An hour or two later, he still had no answers, just a bad headache, and he returned to bed.

In the morning, while waiting for the water to boil for coffee, he gazed at the gas bill envelope propped between the salt and pepper shakers on the table. He contemplated the questions it raised throughout the day and the evening. Old Sacundino used to say that complex questions often responded to simple solutions. None came to him. But he sensed he had come to a major intersection in his life, and that something he could not put into words was at work.

On the Sunday morning of his 34th birthday (November 25th 1971), in the company of friendly birds pecking for worms on the fleshly dug out soil, Alfonso laid bricks for a knee-high retaining wall in his yard.

It was to be his new vegetable garden. He already had lemon and mandarin trees, a fig tree, and a grapevine producing fruit and shade. The weather was warming up, and he had visualised rows of green lettuce and red tomatoes. He wished he had room for other trees to attract lorikeets and not just the grey pigeons, sparrows, and blackbirds. And a hive or two. His mother thought the making of honey was a miracle.

The little radio mumbling to itself on the laundry shelf pipped twelve o'clock. He stopped work, went into the house, boiled water for coffee, and made cheese sandwiches. He ate sitting on an upturned milk crate. A violet and yellow butterfly drifted nearby, and he watched it flutter about the yard. He recalled how the yard looked when he bought the house: the shed, the incinerator, the Hill's hoist, all half-hidden under a melee of weeds, lantana and passion fruit. And later, when it was crowded with friends eating, drinking, and laughing during the housewarming barbecue.

Now, less than six months later, all his friends were gone. Pavel and Claire quarrelled. She packed her belongings and returned to her home city of Adelaide. 'I need her,' Pavel said when he came to say goodbye.

The brothers had started a business of their own. Now they pursued money with the same single-mindedness they once reserved for sex.

Raul had returned to Spain. In his first letter, he wrote that General Franco was 82 and in poor health, and that socialist elements pushing for reform, including divorce, would 'take the country to the cleaners.' In the second letter, he said bad manners were in fashion: his niece had called him an imbecile.

Even the two adjoining neighbours who had reported him to the city council had moved on. The one complaining of noise had a stroke and could barely walk or speak with his twisted mouth. He'd sold the house and gone to live with his daughter in Queensland. Soon after, the other had developed a persistent cough that tormented him day and night for two months before God took pity on him. The house, locked up, waited for the relatives to stop fighting among themselves for its ownership.

He finished eating and took his plate and coffee cup to the kitchen sink. Then he phoned Newtown Building Supplies and ordered a tonne of garden soil. He was alone now, he thought, as he resumed laying bricks. In a way, he always had been alone. But this was a new sadness, difficult to explain. As a child, he'd dreamed of growing up, of magic traps and fishing rods. During his youth and those bleak apprenticeship years, trudging from village to village in the company of good Sacundino, he had dreamed of a kinder way of life. In Australia, it was of a house and a woman.

He had always trusted his dreams. The year the electricity came to the village, frost had ruined their crops, and they had to use their savings to buy grains and potatoes instead of connecting to the new wonder wires. Both his mother and brother were resigned to their house being the only one using an oil lamp.

'Only for a little while,' Mother had said at dinner. But he was not resigned. They looked at the soup in their bowls on hearing that he had dreamed up a solution. And Mother had cried when six months later he won the cash prize for his carved wooden reproduction of Saint Andrés. She had cried again after the light was switched on in the kitchen and in each of their two bedrooms, and laughed in the barn when the hens got up thinking it was already a new day. Dreams had provided a kind of direction, of shelter with a secret tunnel to the future. Now it had all ended.

He mixed another small wheelbarrow of mortar. Just as he finished laying the last row of bricks, the truck arrived to deliver the soil.

'You are quick today, Eusebio,' said Alfonso, opening the back gate.

'We're not busy,' replied Eusebio. 'Any chance of a beer?'

'Of course.'

Alfonso started for the kitchen. Eusebio tipped the soil in the lane against the fence and then came back in. Alfonso handed him a can of beer.

Eusebio took a sip. 'Do you have Mauricio's new telephone number? The boss has work for him.'

'He's gone back.'

'When?'

'In January. He spent Christmas in prison, you know.'

'What for?'

'Fourteen hundred dollars of unpaid parking fines. The brothers and I went to Long Bay on Christmas Eve to get him out, but he refused our offer.'

'Refused?'

'He said he was all right and that six days would go quick and he would prefer we advanced him the money for a one-way ticket back to Cadiz, against his tax return.'

'He was a good man, good wrought iron worker, too. What went wrong?'

'He said Australia had no soul, only overtime, beer, and poker machines. He would rather be poor in Spain than rich here.'

Eusebio lit a cigarette, looked at the house. 'No woman

yet?' he asked.

'No.'

'Can I suggest one?'

'Your mother-in-law?'

'Yes. Plus all the garden soil you want, free. Deal?'

'Let me think about it.'

Eusebio finished the beer, rinsed his mouth with water from the garden hose, and then left.

Alfonso wheelbarrowed the soil into the yard and shovelled it behind the new brickwork. The sun faded as he washed the tools and housed the pavers. He gazed at his new garden and thought of Nancy. She had miraculously arrived in his life on housewarming day. She was the future he had turned his back on. He recalled Raul's words from long ago. 'Divorces and funerals are wives' ultimate weddings.' This, he now believed, was where his world began to unhinge. It set in motion a myriad of things that conspired to derail the relationship. But he no longer felt bitter towards Raul. He had always believed that each man is accountable for his own actions, which became his permanent shadows. Hindsight was a nasty teacher.

'Are you all right, Alfonso?' asked Nick at morning tea.

'I'm fine.'

'You're quiet.'

'You mean quieter,' Barry said.

'He needs a woman,' said Domenico.

'He's too cautious, and too settled in his ways for that,' said Barry.

'He will not survive alone in Australia,' Domenico said as he got up and put the sandwich wrappings in the bin.

Ignoring the bus after work, Alfonso walked home through Hyde Park. The Archibald fountain's multiple rainbows crisscrossed the spray that made momentary bubbles as it splashed into the pool. The water smelled of wet wood. A wedding party gathered on the steps of St Mary's Cathedral for wedding photos. Birds were calling, and the Moreton Bay fig trees in the park were getting new leaves. Nature would renew itself, so what was stopping him from doing the same? He remembered how old Sacundino had respectfully explained to the bishop that three of his eighteenth century chairs would have to be sacrificed to restore the remaining five, because old timber and new timber would not mix. It was the same with his old and new lives arguing in his head. He liked his reasoning and felt his pulse quicken with something resembling hope. He began to walk hurriedly, his sandwich container and thermos rattling in his lunch bag slung over his shoulder. By the time he got to Charles Street, he had decided to contact Nancy and ask her to forgive the hurt he had caused her. Then he wondered if there was still a chance of her taking him back. He felt he was now drawing closer to the core of his confusion. First, he accepted that his behaviour had been influenced by his friend's opinion of women. And more, about Nancy being Australian. And second, his memories could not be erased, but could be shelved in a different section of the mind as he had done with adolescent yearnings, homesickness, and other sacred relics of his life before coming to Australia. No one was just one person, he had read somewhere.

After a shower and a change into fresh clothes, he went to the kitchen, poured himself a glass of wine, peeled two potatoes, which he put in a baking dish with three drumsticks, an onion, and a red capsicum, and lit the oven. Then he picked up the gas bill envelope from the kitchen table, tore it in half, and threw it in the rubbish bin in the cupboard under the sink.

He waited for the clock to read ten minutes past seven, cleared his throat, and dialled Nancy's number.

'Hello,' a man answered.

'May I speak to Nancy Morris, please?'

'She is not here at the moment. Could I ask who is calling?'

'Alfonso.'

'Does she have your phone number?'

'Yes, she has.'

'Very well then,' the man said and hung up.

Alfonso liked the man's pleasant, slow, way of speaking. It would be her father, a maths teacher, Nancy had mentioned once. He felt tense and excited as he washed the dishes and made the sandwiches for work the next day. She was out, and he assumed she would return his call on Saturday or Sunday. Perhaps she was still mad at him and would never call back. Why would she, he thought as he brushed his teeth before going to bed.

The following week, Alfonso purchased assorted seedlings from a Newtown nursery and planted them in the new soil. At nightfall, he watered them and then sat on the stone bench with a glass of wine. The evening hush and the darkened surroundings calmed his inner storms. But now and again a shadow appeared, sometimes shapeless, sometimes in the form of an old man with a sad face and a vague resemblance to himself.

The capsicum plants sprang into flower; the tomatoes followed. In the plant universe, there was reliability and consensus, and he resented it not being the same in his personal life. Was it the price he had to pay for aspiring to a decent life? For rejecting the harshness of poverty, which according to old Sacundino was what we were born for? A

Maltese man at work had once said that the migrants he knew, including himself, ate well, bought houses, and saved money, but deprived of their language, culture, and history, their material riches did not protect them from a life of social and spiritual misery.

His bosses considered him a good carpenter and a reliable worker. Privately, he was proud of having his house and station wagon paid off. He had savings with the Commonwealth Bank and cash in the house, hidden, wrapped in foil in case of a fire. But he didn't have a woman. It had always been his greatest wish to have a woman to share the shopping, the meals, and the bed. Women were everywhere: in supermarkets, on the beaches, at work, at church, on the dance floor, and yet not a single one belonged to him. He had often wondered what it would be like to undress a woman, to be inside her.

More than once he had gone to King's Cross with friends, but he had always found an excuse for avoiding the brothels. One night he went alone. At a bar, he drank a whisky and a beer for courage, and then went to A Touch of Class. As he was about to ring the bell, the door opened and two sailors came out, merry-faced and laughing. He stood aside to let them pass. A moment later, he followed them down the six steps to the street. His brother had been to the city with a gang of bricklayers and had heard of diseases spread by sailors. He told himself there had to be another way.

Later in November Nick gave a party for his parents, who were visiting from Greece. There were eight or ten couples, lots of children running and playing in the house and yard, and loads of meat, some wrapped in leaves. The sun dipped behind the neighbouring roofs, the men began dancing, and Alfonso left. Driving back, he recalled an image of Nick and his attractive wife posing for a photograph, her hand seizing his behind their backs, and another of their lovely young daughters, six and eight, handing out plates with small portions of Greek pastries, and he was envious of his friend.

At home, he changed into shorts and a t-shirt and headed for the backyard, turned on the water tap, and sat on the stone bench. The moon was on the way up, big and white, and the sprinkler shone streaks of silver over the lettuce.

'The only single man at the party,' he said to himself.

His garden was doing well. The tomato plants, firmly secured to wooden stakes, were now almost a metre high. The stakes, made from imperfect tree branches, supported them well. In an imperfect world, there may be no perfect women. But women were no better or worse than men. And if he found that life had no meaning without a woman, marry one. Marry twice, like some people did. Marry three times, if necessary.

'Take your chances and shut up,' he said aloud to himself. A night bird laughed in a tree nearby. He got up and disconnected the hose.

Back in the house, Alfonso drank a glass of water, took a pen from the coffee mug on top of the fridge, and drew another circle on the wall calendar. Nine days, he said to himself, since he had spoken with Nancy's father, and still no phone call. Was the daily recording of the passage of time a futile way of keeping hope alive? He did not know.

The same evening, Alfonso was watching television half-heartedly and reading during the commercials when the phone rang. He got up from the couch to answer it.

'Hello,' he said.

'Father told me you rang,' Nancy said.

'I wished to speak to you.'

'What about?'

'I want to apologise for the way I behaved when you came back from England.'

A silence.

'Do you?'

'Yes. I would like to see you.'

'I work in Parramatta now, Alfonso. Occasionally I go to the city office. Perhaps we could have a coffee during the lunch hour one of these days.'

'I look forward to that.'

'Good. I will get back to you,' she said and hung up.

Alfonso looked at the receiver in his hand. Then he went to the yard and sat on the stone bench and played back Nancy's words. They were not impolite words, but the tone was not warm either. And he felt the loss of his greatest dream as he had never before.

Returning home from work halfway through the week, Alfonso found a police car blocking the entrance to Charles Street, and an ambulance parked nearby. People stood in groups of twos and fours up and down the footpaths, silent or whispering.

'What is going on?' Alfonso asked a man dressed in shorts and thongs with the *Daily Mirror* folded under his arm.

'Old Henry has been dead for a month, slumped in front of his TV.'

Two men dressed in white came out of the house, wheeling a stretcher. Alfonso could make out the contours of the body under a blue blanket that was secured with straps. They eased it into the back of the vehicle, climbed in the front, and drove away. Two officers came out of the house—one a woman—and began asking questions.

Alfonso started walking home, mulling over a memory

of the tall, thin man with a sad, furrowed face sitting on his front porch. Then he thought of himself in his old age, waiting by the letterbox for a letter no one would ever write, walking to the corner shop, arthritic joints creaking like the hinges of an ungreased gate. Ahead, the empty hours between mealtimes and bedtime. Ahead, old dreams, omens, and regrets dying within the coils of his memory. Each day, the same humiliation of being old and alone until death came for him.

'Man dead in house for a month,' read the *Daily Mirror* headline the day after. 'Our society doesn't care,' said the *Sun-Herald*. There was speculation about the man's life, his family, his friends, or lack of them, on the inside pages.

Alfonso would not be surprised if there were rumours and speculation if he too died alone. How come he wasn't married? Was there something wrong with him? Did he favour men? His friends had created opportunities for him to meet women, but no matter how well it all started, it dwindled to nothing.

The manner of Henry's death haunted him. What if he got ill again and died? Would anyone notice his absence? What would happen to the house and the tools? Where and by whom would he be buried? Had he died back home, he would be buried in the village graveyard, sheltered by the cypress trees, with his name incised on the headstone and remembered. In death, he would be met by friends already there. Others would follow. In the village, people believed that the need for companionship in death was the same as in life. But in Sydney, he would most likely be cremated and quickly forgotten.

The panic of loneliness played in his mind for several days. And he feared being marginalised, like so many other migrants he had met. Then, watching TV one evening, he saw a character sitting quietly at home, feeling sad and bitter, thinking that life was passing him by, and before the program was over, he knew he had to go out and socialise. So when it rained a few days later and work stopped, he went to Grace Brothers on Broadway and bought two shirts, nylon socks, an Italian-made jacket, and two pairs of trousers.

In the bedroom, he unpacked his new clothes and laid them on the bed. To make room in the wardrobe, he took out his old jackets and trousers—some so narrow that he almost needed a shoehorn to get into them, others as wide as women's skirts. These garments were intimate witnesses to his past, he thought, as he slowly folded them and placed them on the top shelf. Each article of clothing was a document of feelings and fashions of the day, much like the rings in a tree trunk record weather conditions.

Alfonso walked to Paddy's Market for the weekly shopping. He was preoccupied with some technical aspect of his work. He was also thinking how good it would be if Nancy was waiting for him at home and he could tell her about it.

In Charles Street, he put the groceries away, changed his clothes, and stretched out on the couch to rest a bit and to separate the week's routines from the weekend's.

When he woke up one hour later, it was raining. It was a gentle, nourishing rain, like spring rain in the village, he thought. He liked it. His plants would, too. It also meant he would not go out tonight. Who would expose his perfectly ironed new pants, jacket, and fine Italian shoes to the rain? He knew straightaway the excuse was flawed, but at the edges of his mind there was a growing conviction that club hopping was no longer an attractive way to spend a Saturday evening.

I'll go out tomorrow, he said to himself as a compromise. He would go up the road to the church that had the Spanish-speaking priest. Since the drowning of Amador and his girlfriend Carmen, for which he blamed the church, his faith had not recovered. But he would enjoy walking there and back while trying to view the world in another way. There was also the informal gathering for coffee or tea in the small courtyard after Mass.

Sometimes he exchanged glances with Marisa, and occasionally they had a chat. Long ago, there had been the beginning of something. They had danced and gone to the beach. Once she had cooked artichokes and, sitting across from him at her tiny kitchen table, she showed him how to eat them by using his teeth to scrape the leaves all the way to the tender and moist heart. Then he had bought a house, unaware that it needed a new roof, that the neighbours had to be appeased, that termites had reduced the timbers to dust. Money was short, and he had stopped going out on the weekends. A year-and-a-half later, she married a man from Argentina. Now she was a widow, in mourning clothes, with lots of grey hair, ashen skin, and sadness in her eyes, but as shapely as ever. He remained concerned for her and wished her heart would mend.

He got up, made a cup of coffee and took it upstairs, stepped out into the verandah, and sat on Guapo's old wrought iron chair, still showing paint and other scars from the house renovations, which he meant to restore to honour his intriguing old friend. He looked up at the grey sky stretching into the distance, and then down, noticing that there were no cars on the street or birds or people about. Even the cheerful family of crickets living near the front gate was silent. It was all very still, weird in a way, he thought. And that was when he saw Nancy standing under the branches of the tree in front of the house, drenched, her dress clinging to her body, just as she had stood that terrible morning less than three months ago.

After some hesitation, startled but clear-headed, he raced downstairs to welcome her into the house and out of the rain. He opened the front door and closed it almost immediately, then stood with his back against the wall. What is happening to me? Am I going insane, he asked himself?

After a while he got busy, which was a habit he fell into when he was troubled by something. He retrieved the coffee cup from the verandah, changed the bed sheets, and threw his dirty clothes in the washing machine. Slowly and meticulously, he cleaned the shower recess, its glass door, and the toilet and mopped the kitchen and bathroom floors. He then brought out the ingredients for making a Spanish omelette for dinner. Night came into the house. Outside, the silent rain was still falling.

The mass had just started when Julián slid into Alfonso's pew. Alfonso followed Father José's Mass rituals and thought about Julian. He was from the early days; they had gone out to clubs together. He had taught Alfonso and the twins the basics of chess and dominoes.

'What are you doing here?' Alfonso asked him the moment they stepped out of the church afterwards. 'I heard you had had enough of repairing bulldozers for BHP and had gone back for good.'

'That was the intention,' replied Julián, 'but wages were not that good, and my old friends had new families. The old ways had gone, and we did not have much in common anymore.'

'Where are you staying?'

'The People's Palace in Pitt Street.'

'You can stay at my place.'

'No point. I'm leaving tomorrow.'

'Where to?'

'Mount Isa. Let's go for lunch.'

They walked to Central Station and then along George Street to the Spanish Club. They ordered two vermouths and a plate of olives. At the counter, they were joined by Ramiro and Antonio, both of them pleased to see Julián. After another round of drinks, they went to the dining room on the first floor. They sat at their old table under the Velazquez portrait, generally known as the bachelor's table. It was there that they had gathered every Saturday night to dine and plan their evening.

'Remember the Saturday nights at the Concordia Club?' Antonio asked, after the waiter had taken their orders.

'Luck was not at my side there,' Julián said.

'You did well at The Phoenician Club,' said Alfonso.

'He was a king of the cougars,' Ramiro said. 'There were rumours that he was raffled every Friday night.'

'I did what I had to do. And I did it properly. That is why I could always go back for more,' Julián said.

'What happened to your Australian friend from the Department of Motor Transport?' Antonio asked. 'You both could have made a name for yourselves as mass murderers.'

'I disagree,' Julián said. 'All I did was arrange the introductions. You gave the man the details, paid the money, and a week later you had your driver's licence. Of course, you would still have to learn to drive.' They all laughed.

They ordered another bottle of wine and mused over the days when they were fresh in the country, when there was always energy to work and play. Julián sought news of the brothers. Ramiro wanted to know what happened to the tailor who wore sunglasses in nightclubs.

The restaurant dining room was nearly full, mostly with couples. There were Luisa and Anton and their children at a table nearby, and Ignacio and Elisa with a couple he didn't know by the fireplace. There was a birthday party in the mezzanine. A man stopped by their table on his way out and told a joke about perennial bachelors on the road to decline.

'I heard the club got a new weekend band,' Julián said when the man left.

'About time,' said Antonio.

'Won't make any difference,' Ramiro said. 'Only couples, yesterday's flowers, and desperados attend the weekend dances now.'

'You are thinking of Conchita,' said Antonio. 'You haven't forgotten her rejection.'

'I am not. Have a look tonight, Julián, and you'll agree with me.'

They shared the bill and went to the ground floor bar for coffee and brandy. Afterwards, Ramiro and Julián left to visit a friend. Alfonso and Antonio played a game of dominoes with two acquaintances of Antonio's whose wives were playing the poker machines.

There were ten men in the cards room, most of them unshaven, unkempt, their faces betraying failure, and under that failure, seething anger. When he commented on their gloomy companions, Antonio said that they were rejected husbands with children and ex-wives scattered in the suburbs. They were passing the hours in collective despair. Some had given up work and devoted all their energies to being miserable. One had gone crazy.

'And there will be more,' he added.

'Why?' Alfonso asked.

'It appears that marrying Australian women is not working.'

At about four o'clock the game was over and Alfonso left the club. The air was clean. There were hardly any cars or pedestrians on George Street. The city's cheerless Sunday aspect, he thought. He knew it well, having always worked in the city. He had seen old buildings become holes in the ground, new ones rising slowly skyward. He had seen the dry-cleaning workers in Park Street sweating through summer and winter, the coiffured women toiling behind the gleaming display windows of Angus and Coote, the jewellers, the closing down of the one-eyed butcher's shop in Pitt Street. With time, the look of the sky, weather inflections, odours, sounds, degrees of light and shadow, even moods and thoughts had settled themselves in his memory alongside the old ones of village paths, puddles, cliffs, creek beds, trees, and bridges he knew like old friends.

At Chinatown the shops were open, and the air was thick with the smell of spices. Dry goods on the pavement. Golden ducks hung by their necks in restaurant windows. Ahead of him, a couple and their two children came out of a restaurant called Marigold. She had shiny black hair, and he wore a white shirt, black trousers, black shoes, and white socks. Alfonso wondered if the white socks were a mistake or a new fashion. Neither, perhaps. The Chinese, Arabs, Indians, and others had their own way of dressing and feeding themselves. His old friend, the tailor, would say that Australia was like a zoo.

The Chinese family got into a white Holden. The children were arguing in the back; the parents were laughing. Did that Chinese man come to Australia alone? Alfonso wondered.

He crossed Elizabeth Street. Raul's words came to his mind: 'Marry one of your own. Although she may have no schooling, she can knead her bread, sew and cook, obey, and appreciate hot and cold water in the taps.'

What did Raul know about relationships other than dominance and submission? Alfonso asked himself. Raul was wrong, Alfonso thought. Marriage in Australia was played by a different set of rules. Here, every woman had hot and cold water in the house and a washing machine. Respect had to be earned and then maintained, not simply bought with convenience. Then what were the basic elements to prevent a marriage from going stale? Was it physical attraction burning bright? Was it intelligent choice? Was it just a game in which he should follow his feelings and trust his luck?

At home, he went straight to his bedroom, opened the verandah's French doors, and gazed at the sparse, moving clouds and the street emptiness below, painted with afternoon shadows in the distinctive Sunday stillness. He undressed, put his new clothes in the wardrobe, and lay on the bed. Now and then a breeze coming off the street felt good on his body.

The company of old friends had cheered him up, but the bitter masks of the card players undid it. His mind began reliving the sickening scenes from Pascual's suicide and his own failure to persuade him to move into Charles Street until he could cope with his troubles. They were followed by images of the silent, homeless men—living ghosts with social security numbers, someone called them—that inhabited the dark alleys of Woolloomooloo and other places that made up the city derelicts' territory. All knitted together against a background of hurt, relationships, and the silhouettes of women.

Determined not to dwell on it, not to abandon his new resolve to reconcile with reality and make something of his future life, he went out to the yard and watered the plants. He lay on the stone bench with one hand behind his head, looking at the stars coming out across the sky. He fell asleep. In a dream he saw Eulalia, Carla, Nancy, and others whose names escaped him, standing nearby, neither questioning nor accusing. Their expressions were friendly, yet he perceived sadness. And he sensed they were the ghostly observers of a foolish man.

He awoke to the phone ringing in the house and he hurried to answer it.

'Alfonso,' he said.

It was Nancy.

'I simply have no time to see you, Alfonso,' she said. Her boss had gone on holiday and the person doing her old job was sick. In ten days, she and her father would drive to Tamworth to spend Christmas and New Year's Eve with his twin sister and her family. She had appreciated his call. Could she ask him a question?

'Yes,' Alfonso said.

'Was there a woman with you when I knocked on your door?'

'No,' he said.

Then she wished him Merry Christmas and hung up.

For a long moment, he looked at the receiver still in his hand, and then he poured a glass of wine and returned to the stone bench. The ghosts of his earlier dream had been replaced by the shadows of clouds drifting across a bright moon on its way up.

'What else can you expect from such conduct?' he said to himself aloud. But he was grateful to her for freeing him from a web of superstition, and for making him aware of prejudice and of his status as a half-outsider, a sort of double-consciousness, and other things that he would not otherwise have permitted himself to understand. Knowing who he was still eluded him, but he clearly felt that he was a different person from the one he had been before meeting her, although he couldn't say why.

In early December 1971 the company's Christmas party was held at the Camperdown Travelodge Hotel. Alfonso sat at a table with Nick and Domenico and their wives. Two tables away sat Sandra with her tall, thin-necked husband, a surveyor. She smiled at him. He smiled back. She was a year younger than he was, a little taller, with red cheeks and rich blue eyes. She worked in accounts. It was she who had supplied him with a letter for the bank, confirming his earnings when he bought the house. Once, before she was married, they had danced together at a Christmas party. They went to the cinema and the beach several times after that. One evening in his car, outside her apartment in Kirribilli, she asked him, 'Have you ever been with a frigid woman?'

'No,' he said. At home he looked up 'frigid' and found: 'A woman having difficulty in becoming sexually excited.'

As December progressed, the shop windows dressed up for Christmas. People carried shopping bags and wore a lighter expression in their faces. He became withdrawn and pensive. Christmas, for some reason, was when Alfonso ached for his father most. He wished to have known him, how he died, where he was buried.

His thoughts reverted to the Christmases of his childhood. They would kill a pig, whose death scream reached him still, then cut it up and dip it in salt for a couple of weeks.

The blood pancakes, the liver, kidneys, and brain were a welcome if brief respite from the monotony of their narrow menu. The postman would bring an airmail envelope. It would contain a Christmas card and a cheque from an old relative in Cuba with a good memory and a big heart until Fidel Castro killed both. Mother would go to town with the cheque and buy enough corduroy material for a pair of trousers for Alfonso and his brother, as well as dress material for herself, and oil and saffron to colour the potatoes on Sunday. The village boys would make snowmen and chase foxes and rabbits trapped in the snow. Those recollections made him feel at once happy and sad.

On Christmas Day, Alfonso placed a tray with a chicken and potatoes in the oven. The phone rang three or four times before he took it off the hook without answering it. He had already politely refused invitations and did not want to do it again. He was in no mood to handle the company of warring uncles and aunties at Barry's, or the disapproving mothers-in-law at Domenico's, or Nick's house where the English language hardly crossed the front door and there was no end to the traditional Greek dishes, song, and dance.

He set the table the way his mother did for a holiday, regretting that he did not have a linen tablecloth. Outside it was hot. He lay on the couch and tried to read. Unable to focus, he got up and wandered about the house. In every corner of the world, in the middle of the day or night, families would be gathered in their houses, bonded by recollections of births and deaths, in photos on the walls, crockery in the cupboards, old letters in the drawers. In his life, on his walls, and in his rooms, there was only silence.

Between Christmas and New Year, he did not leave the house. In the cool of the morning, in the shade of the grapevine, he worked restoring an old hallstand he had found at a garage sale. When it become too hot, he went inside and read, slept, or watched TV. Towards evening, he watered the garden, drank a glass of wine, and regained a measure of peace. He was not a homeless man; he was not sick in hospital; he was not at war.

'I have a job, I have friends, and one day I will have a family,' he said to himself. But these were just isolated bubbles of relief. Never had he felt so alone, his past so heavy. And he began to consider defeat.

Chapter Two

On the morning of New Year's Eve, Alfonso received an unusually large bundle of commercial mail held together by a thick red rubber band. He took it to the coffee table in the living room, lay on the couch, and started looking at the items for sale in each catalogue. He had no intention of buying anything, but he was tired and his state of mind was no good for anything else. Halfway through the pile, he came across a white envelope with his name and address written in blue, which he instantly recognised as Nancy's handwriting.

He felt strong apprehension as he gazed at it and the four-day-old postmark over the photo of the young queen in the corner. He turned over the envelope and read Nancy's Tamworth address. When the envelope started trembling in his hands, he went to the kitchen and from the cutlery drawer he selected the potato peeling knife and slid it along the top end of the envelope. Inside there was a note.

'Dear Alfonso. Your phone appears to be out of order. The film *Walkabout* is showing at the Valhalla in Glebe. Would you like to see it? Call me after January 6th. Happy New Year, Nancy.'

Alfonso walked to the yard and smiled at the row of birds on the power line and at the children riding their new bicycles in the lane. Tears burned in his eyes.

Later that day, Alfonso walked to the city to dine with friends at Don Quixote restaurant. Twilight was fading, and it was hot and humid, with dense clouds hanging low. Earlier in the day, he had considered not going out, but then he thought of his first months and his first friends in Australia, and their pledge to always meet on New Year's Eve.

José, Ramiro, Martin, and their wives were already in the restaurant's bar. Alfonso shook hands with the men and kissed the women.

Ramiro handed him a beer.

'You are looking very smart, Alfonso,' said Celia, Martin's wife, as she straightened his tie.

They had another round of drinks before they were shown to their table. The crowded, noisy restaurant made conversation difficult, which suited Alfonso's restrained new excitement. Nancy's note, he reasoned, did not necessarily mean that she would take him back. Perhaps the gulf between them would now be impossible to bridge. But the gesture for some form of reconciliation was there, and he treasured it.

The waiter kept filling his wine glass. The entrée of prawn and oysters was good, and the roast suckling pig excellent. After dinner, they walked to the Spanish Club and ordered two bottles of champagne. Acquaintances joined in, and they ordered more champagne. They all yelled at the stroke of midnight, reminisced, and laughed at themselves. Alfonso danced with his friends' wives in turn. Strange, he thought, that he had never danced with Nancy.

It was long after midnight when he left the club. The air was cool and the empty streets glistened, newly washed from an evening storm. He walked along George Street in the direction of Broadway, going home the long way. But his legs were light, his thoughts were calm, and he did not care. He wished his friends' happiness could last forever. He wondered where he and Nancy would be in twelve months' time.

When he came to a small park near Central Station, he felt a strange urge to cross the street and go in. His shiny new shoes sank a little in the wet grass, and he thought of turning back, but he sat on a bench instead. His eyelids became heavy, and the noise of revellers and the wailing of police cars faded.

He was six or seven. It was spring, bees busy in the flowers, birds nesting. He and his mother were walking home from doing the washing in the river when, in a small clearing next to the trail, he saw a brown snake slowly writhing out of its skin. His mother took the laundry basket off her head and placed it on the ground. She held his hand, and they both watched until the snake was totally free and it had slithered away into the bushes.

'Lucky snake,' Mother said after they resumed walking.

'Why, Mamá?'

'New dress every year.'

Alfonso woke to the rattle of an early train. He felt the gentle summer rain streaming down his face. He opened his eyes in time to see a translucent woman and a boy on the edge of the park, smiling and waving goodbye and slowly fading into the morning like ghosts in a film.

He got up and set off for Charles Street. At home he took off his shoes and socks in the hallway and dropped the rest of his dripping garments in the living room. Then, naked, in the dawn light that was now forcing its way through the rain clouds into the house, he wandered from room to room, like a traveller returning from a long journey.

Félix Calvino was born in Galicia, on the northwest coast of Spain, and grew up on a farm. To avoid military service under General Franco, he went to England where he worked and studied English, his third language. (His other languages are Galician and Spanish.) He migrated to Australia in the later '60s, settled in Sydney and worked in the travel, restaurant, and wine industry. In 1996 he moved to Melbourne and a year later, a long-held ambition for a tertiary education was fulfilled when he was admitted to the University of Melbourne.
There he studied English and Spanish as components of his Bachelor of Arts degree. In 2012, Félix graduated with a Master of Philosophy in the field of creative writing from the University of Queensland.

MORE FINE FICTION IN THE PRESS ON SERIES

1. Peter Corris, *Wishart's Quest*, ISBN 978 1 921509 54 4
2. Michael Wilding, *The Prisoner of Mt Warning*, ISBN 978 1 921509 56 8
3. Phillip Edmonds, *Leaving Home with Henry*, ISBN 978 1 921509 55 1
4. Inez Baranay, *With The Tiger*, ISBN 978 1 921509 57 5
5. Ross Fitzgerald & Trevor L Jordan, *Fools' Paradise*, ISBN 978 1 921509 58 2
6. Victoria Thompson, *City of Longing*, ISBN 978 1 921875 36 6
7. Peter Corris, *The Colonial Queen*, ISBN 978 1 921875 31 1
8. Michael Wilding, *The Magic of It*, ISBN 978 1 921875 37 3
9. Morris Lurie, *Hergesheimer Hangs In*, ISBN 978 1 921875 34 2
10. Garry Disher, *Play Abandoned*, ISBN 978 1 921875 33 5
11. Inez Baranay, *Always Hungry*, ISBN 978 1 921875 30 4
12. Ian Callinan, *Dislocation*, ISBN 978 1 921875 38 0
13. Félix Calvino, *A Hatful of Cherries*, ISBN 978 1 740971 67 6
14. James Murray, *Shark City*, ISBN 978 1 921875 35 9
15. Peter Corris, *Standing in the Shadow*, ISBN 978 1 921875 32 8
16. Michael Wilding, *Asian Dawn*, ISBN 978 1 921875 39 7
17. Colin Talbot, *Ah, Sweet Mystery*, ISBN 978 1 921875 93 9
18. Morris Lurie, *Hergesheimer in the Present Tense*, ISBN 978 1 921875 95 3
19. Michael Wilding, *Little Demon*, ISBN 978 1 921875 94 6
20. Félix Calvino, *Alfonso*, isbn 978-1-925003-20-8